fearfully
and
Wonderfully
MADE

a novel

Donald Jordan

Negative Capability
PRESS

ISBN 978-0-9986777-3-6
Library of Congress Control Number: 2020915164

Published by Negative Capability Press
150 Du Rhu Drive, #2202
Mobile, AL 36608
www.negativecapabilitypress.org
facebook.com/negativecapabilitypress

To my friend, Jimmy Elder, who remembers the age of innocence.

1

We didn't know what was in the old garage but suspected it must be instruments of torture and parts of dead bodies. At least twice a day I had to walk or ride my bicycle past it, and in winter when returning home from my paper route after dark I was terrified to pass the haunted garage. I held my breath, pumped furiously and didn't exhale until reaching the streetlight a block away.

It wasn't as if the dilapidated old garage was sealed off behind a house or fence. The sagging doors came right up to the sidewalk, secured by a heavy padlock. Along the sidewalk from the garage ran a vine-snarled fence on rotting posts, and behind the fence was a gloomy two-story frame house. High weeds and scraggly trees guarded the dark rear porch. The rooms of the big house remained mostly unlit, and the dingy curtains were pulled tightly over the windows. Some people said that the upstairs floors were never occupied, but I knew better. Once when I was hurrying by I glanced up to see the corner of a curtain drop.

One summer my friend Malcolm Hughley, who was two years older but only one grade higher, and who had already unlocked all the secrets of life, seized my arm and dared me to look through the crack in the rotting garage doors.

"You look yourself," I said.

"I did, when we first heard something was in there."

"And what did you see?"

"I'm not sure. But it doesn't matter. Whatever it is can change forms at will."

"Well, I'm not going near that place."

"Why not?"

"You know why not. I could be sucked inside. You'd find my arms or head, maybe."

"You're not a coward, are you?"

It was a bright sunlit afternoon. Cars were streaming along the street. All the way up the sidewalk Malcolm jostled and harassed me. "Sooner or later, Skeeter, you have to look. I won't always be with you."

Finally he wore me down. While he waited about thirty yards away, I crept forward and pressed one eye against the crack in the doors. Bright as it was outside, I was amazed by the darkness inside. But for a single sliver of light, there was total blackness. I could smell a faint odor of rot and decay. Then as my eye adjusted, I caught a single pinpoint of light drilling a knothole in the siding, and this light struck upon the left shoulder, forearm and naked breast of a human figure.

With a horrified cry I ran. Malcolm ran, too, for though he had not seen what I saw he couldn't mistake the urgency with which my panicky legs transported me. At last when we could run no more he caught my arm and jerked me to a halt. "What did you see, Skeeter!"

"A body!" I gasped.

"I knew it!"

"Have you seen him, too?"

"How do you know it's a him? Maybe it's a dead woman! A naked woman!"

His face was flushed red, and in his eyes was a look of horrified fascination. We ran on, he dropped off at his house on the corner, and I hurried on up Schaul Street to the little brick home where we lived.

For two days I couldn't bring myself to tell my family about my snooping. At that point in our lives my whole family's greatest fear was that my father might lose his job; we could be thrown out of our house and there would be nowhere to go. I had little doubt that the spooky old garage could reach out its evil hand to threaten our family with displacement and hunger. Finally in my ten-year-old anxiety I could hold back no longer. "Malcolm made me," I defended myself. "I just looked through the crack in the doors."

To my amazement they demonstrated little interest.

Finally my older brother Mat said, "If you saw anything, which I doubt, it was some tools or boxes. Maybe an old dress form or a mannequin."

"It was real!" I cried. "I could smell it!"

"Every old garage smells." Mat gave me one long look of disgust. I knew he hated me. "Scaredy-cat."

I clamped my mouth shut and said nothing more. Of course a mannequin dropped onto a discarded old chair would discredit my fears of evil origin. But what I had seen had to be something alive, if not human. I knew this because just before I turned to run I detected the faint glow of a cigarette.

* * *

Mat and I found out about the threat to our family's survival by accident. We had just left the supper table one night as Mama and Daddy remained talking. Our cramped house was so small that even though they lowered their voices, conversation carried through the thin walls. We heard, "...you could be arrested..." and "the store might be closed..." and we both stopped to listen.

"I hope it won't come to that," Daddy said.

"He's a criminal and you're a party to it." Mama's tone was strained. "What would we do without a job?"

Mat turned back into the dining room and I followed. At sixteen he believed he had a right to know everything, and though he was six years older, I had a paper route, earned my own money and thought that in a way I was just as old as he.

"What are you talking about? We want to know," we said.

Finally they let us in on what was going on. Mr. Blaise Montgomery, Daddy's employer, had finessed his way into the Fort Benning, Georgia, Contracting Office and was receiving contracts for repainting hundreds of barracks, officers' quarters, mess halls, and housing on the Post. By bribing certain officers and inspectors he was enriching himself at taxpayers' expense. He had his crews apply a primer and one coat of paint when two were specified; he thinned paint and glazed over rotting siding which was supposed to be replaced; he negotiated change orders for additional work which was never done. If Daddy kept quiet about all this he was an accessory to the criminal activity and a betrayer of his conscience. If he confronted Mr. Montgomery—Monty, Daddy called him—he would probably lose his job.

"But Daddy has to tell the truth!" I stuck my nose in.

Mama looked at me solemnly. "Don't you breathe a word of this, Skeeter. It'll only make matters worse."

As Mat and I left the room I looked at him for reassurance but as usual he wasn't interested in giving me the time of day.

"It's the garage," I muttered.

"What?"

"Never mind. You never listen to me anyway."

The sinister old garage was just three blocks from us and I knew evil was never constrained by time or distance. If Daddy lost his job, where would we sleep, how would we eat? What would we do about medicine for my little sister Joanie? Our small house on Schaul Street was nothing compared to the houses on my paper route off Hilton Avenue, but we were proud of it. Mother was a born homemaker. She was an insecure and shy person and the house was her fortress and refuge. With our two-year-old Joanie sick, with meals to plan and prepare, with Mat and me to deal with, she hardly ever sat down.

I knew Daddy couldn't just say, "It's none of my business," or, "I do only as I'm told." He was too honest and he couldn't quit. With all his hard work day and night he couldn't seem to make ends meet. Still, he never gave up. He never stopped trying, and sometimes I thought his capability exceeded the circumstances he'd fallen into. It hurt me to see him trudge off to work each morning, dreading his day, then at night and on weekends sawing and hammering himself into exhaustion on some renovation or room addition, or crawling under dreadfully cold, wet, friendless houses to repair oil floor furnaces to make a little extra money.

* * *

My baby sister Joanie was playing around in the grass at our back door. I was in the kitchen with Mama when Marshall, the delivery man for City Market, came through the door and placed two brown bags of groceries on our table. He removed his cap and mumbled, "Miz Harding, Miz Copeland wants to know if you can pay a little on your account today."

A deep flush swept through my mother's face. "Tell Mrs. Copeland I'll settle my account next week, Marshall." She fished into her pocket and handed him a dime. He accepted it humbly and hurried back to his truck.

I helped put away the purchases. The cabinets on either side of the window could only hold the cups and dishes, and the cabinet in the kitchen corner was jammed with half empty jars and bottles. The best we could do was arrange cans and boxes neatly on the counter space beside the sink. We had emptied one bag and begun the second when Mama burst into tears. She stumbled into the dining room, pulled out a chair and dropped her head into her hands.

I ran to the bedroom closet where I kept a cigar box containing the savings from my paper route. I brought it and set it on the table before her. She shook her head dismally. "I won't take your money, Skeeter."

"I don't mind. You need it."

"You don't understand."

I understood more than she thought. She hardly ever said anything but seldom a day passed that I didn't see her in tears over the grocery bill, the pharmacy bill, shoes for Joanie. I knew she was worried about Daddy losing his job, about mounting medical needs and about me, too. She thought ten years old was too young to have one of the hardest paper routes in Columbus.

She pulled herself up from the table and went back to the kitchen. With her slight frame, short brown hair, deep-set eyes and prominent brow, she had, people said, the shape and movements of a young girl. Her fingers were agile and confident with sewing needles and piano keys, but she was shy and self-conscious. Nearly every Sunday before church she asked Daddy and sometimes Mat and me about the back of her hair. "Is it sticking out? Does it need brushing again?"

"It looks fine."

"I don't want people noticing my hair."

My mother's father had taken off when she was a child, leaving my grandmother to raise seven children. His name was never mentioned around our house. All I knew about him was that he was a master craftsman, cabinet maker and carpenter. In our dining room was a beautiful prayer scroll, emblazoned with poetic calligraphy, the only piece I'd ever seen that he carved. How my grandmother held a family of seven children together with no help I didn't know. I assumed she must have been a woman of courage, and that my mother inherited her bravery.

No matter what anyone said or did to Mother, she refused to hold a grudge. "You can never tell what someone is thinking," she'd say, or, "You don't know why so and so did that."

At the kitchen sink she washed her face, then finished arranging the groceries. Whether there would be money to meet the promise she'd made to Marshall was yet to be seen.

* * *

I was standing in our living room looking out the window. A cold blowing rain howled across our front porch. Outside the window my bicycle stood like a wind-lashed steed. I hoped it wouldn't let me down today. A burning fist clutched my stomach. If it weren't for the money I wouldn't set foot into such a horrid day.

Mama said, "You can't go out in weather like this, Skeeter. Your customers will understand."

"No, they won't. They expect their papers to be delivered."

I went into the kitchen and made myself a banana and peanut butter sandwich, and then sat at the dining room table eating slowly. As a great crash of thunder and hard, biting pellets of rain whipped down, I was filled with dread. I shivered, hoping the storm would break.

My route was a maze of long, looping streets, houses set far back from the roads, up-slopes, twisting descents and steep hills. In weather like this it could be brutal, especially when I was afraid that my old Schwinn might collapse at any moment. I wondered if I'd ever be able to get a new bike. For the thousandth time I wished Daddy had a secure, well-paying job. But seeing him plow off to work each morning, I felt I had no choice but to do my part with this paper route.

When I had waited as long as I dared, I got up and put on as many clothes as I could manage and still retain some mobility. It was just about impossible to ride a bicycle with a raincoat, just as difficult to pull papers out of the tight canvas bag wearing gloves. So I wore neither. As I slipped on a wide-brimmed rain hat and started out, Mama gave me a look of regret.

The instant I stepped onto the porch, shards of cold air sliced across my nose, hands, and fingers. I trembled with worry and then mounted my bike and hit the street. Before I reached the corner I was soaked. There was practically no light in the sky, even though it was four o'clock in the afternoon. Street lights flickered and glowed eerily in the cutting north wind.

By the time I reached Wynnton School, the drop-off station for the

Ledger, I couldn't have been more miserable. But I had to fold and bag my papers and get them to my customers. I envied those carriers whose mothers or fathers drove them around on days like this, and others who rode bikes but could finish in an hour or so. I had one of the largest and most difficult routes in Columbus, a combination of two routes, really, which I'd talked my manager into, needing the money.

I secured the bag on the handlebars and plunged out into the rain. Up Wildwood Avenue I pedaled, pumping through half-frozen puddles. I plowed around Stark Avenue and hit Wildwood again, then looped down to Hilton where the mansions were far back from the street. On rainy days papers had to be put behind screen doors or under *porte-cocheres*, and just to pedal up one of Hilton's long driveways and place the paper in a dry place was a time-consuming task.

From time to time the rain let up, then lashed down again with a vengeance. The jacket and sweater I'd put on were soggy, my eyelids nearly frozen. Out in the open, with no houses or trees to break the wind, the gusts cut like blades of ice. I sneaked up onto a small covered porch, dropped the *Ledger* behind the screen door, and then stood partially sheltered, looking forlornly down at my bike. The worst thing that could happen to me on a day like this was a slipped chain, a flat tire, or some other malfunction. My frozen fingers would never allow the dexterity for repairs. My canvas bag was soaked through. Most of the papers had wet edges and a renewed panic seized me. It was getting darker. Houses stood cold and isolated. Only a window here or there let out an occasional glimmer of light. The great oaks ranking the sidewalks stood stark and rigid, brittle limbs beaten by wind, upper canopies sucking in dreary light.

A lone panel truck came by, tires swishing geysers of gutter water, headlights transforming hard bullets of rain into silver crystals. I could imagine the inside of the cab to be warm and secure. I watched it pass, then the street grew lifeless again. Not even a dog ventured out. It was a howling ghost street that seemed to distance me from anything comfortable and friendly. After a few minutes I steeled myself and slipped back out to my bike. I couldn't give up, I needed the money, and self-pity would earn me no escape. Street by street, I didn't quit until every paper was delivered.

I slipped a half-wet *Ledger* behind the last screen door and then, remembering how terrifying the possessed old garage would be on a black night like this, I pedaled an extra block out of the way to get home. When finally I rode back into our driveway and trudged into the house like a drowned rat, my mother burst into tears. "Your Daddy's been looking for you …"

I hadn't realized they would worry about me. I'd been managing this route for over a year now.

"I'm sorry you have to do this, Skeeter."

"It's okay. I don't mind."

I had been gone nearly four hours. The evening was pitch dark, ice forming along the edges of puddles and in street gutters, and Daddy had come home and immediately set out to find me. What good this would have done, I didn't know. I couldn't have abandoned my route, perhaps he hoped only to reassure himself of my safety. I wasn't surprised that he hadn't found me. Many times I left the streets and cut through side yards and backyards, to save time.

Standing on the hearth I shed my coat and clothes, then went into the bath where Mama had drawn a tub of hot water, and eased myself in. There was an instantaneous burning all up and down. It would have been better to begin with a cold bath and warm gradually, but in time my skin adjusted to the heat. I relaxed and lay soaking, eyes closed, trying to forget my day. Still, when at last I climbed from the tub and dried off, my arms, legs and chest were beet red and stinging, and didn't really feel normal again until later that night when I sank exhausted under the deep covers of bed.

As my eyes grew heavy I heard Mama and Daddy talking. They were trying to figure out a way to pay Miss Copeland at City Market — which meant that no matter how hard the winter days were I had to try to earn enough money to help out, and to get a new bike. If my old Schwinn failed me, and sooner or later it was bound to, I'd be stuck just as Daddy was. I had to get a new bicycle and I had to stop being afraid.

2

My brother Mat thought I was a nuisance—a ten-year-old, thorn-in-the-flesh nuisance. As far as I could tell, nothing satisfied him more than giving me a rap with his fist or abusing me verbally. He wasn't afraid of anything, and my fear of so many things commanded his contempt.

Mat was mad a lot. Why, I'm not certain. Perhaps because we were so poor and many of the boys he ran with were well off. I really think, though, that it was because he was so skinny and good-looking. As a child he'd contracted malaria, consequently he tended to be vulnerable to viruses and colds, and he could never gain weight. He was self-conscious about his size, tried to make up for it with a quick temper, and I was his most accessible victim.

How concerned he was about Daddy losing his job I couldn't tell. Mat seldom expressed his feelings. Probably under the right circumstances he would have ground Mr. Blaise Montgomery into the dirt. His fury could be swift and deadly to the extent that boys older and heavier were shocked senseless. Before Mat turned the paper route over to me he was viciously attacked by three boys, drifters and no-goods, on the Wynnton School grounds. We wouldn't have known about it if some stranger hadn't telephoned Daddy. The boys, from the poorest part of town, had been bumming around when they spotted Mat getting ready to deliver his papers. They jumped him and tied him to a tree with wires that held bundles of newspapers together. A man walking his dog discovered him and set him loose. "He never said a word," the gentleman reported. "I left him picking up the scattered papers."

Mama was horrified, Daddy stunned, and I shuddered at the rage I knew Mat felt. I was afraid someday he would get himself maimed and battered if not killed. But it wasn't really clear to us what had happened until he came home hours late from his paper route. His face was closed tight, his lips thin, his jaw clenched, and only after much persuasion did he explain the raw red marks on his wrists and the thin cord of chaffing around his neck. If The Good Samaritan who freed him had not gone to the trouble to reach the route manager at the *Ledger* who gave him our telephone number, we never would have heard a word about it.

Mat would not tip the scales at more than a hundred twenty pounds. He had black hair and cold blue eyes, fine features and a delicate face. At fifteen, he had hated being a pretty boy but realized it worked in his favor with girls. They were drawn to him like honeybees.

It was probably Mat's appearance that made him the subject of harassment. How many times I had seen boys thirty pounds heavier driven to their knees by the deadly sting of his fists I didn't know.

With a cold, fixed expression, he finally told us the facts about his encounter with the cruel boys at school. He swore he didn't know who they were, but I had an idea he did. And a month later I saw him begin his calculated retribution. We were riding together around Lake Bottom, the park where the Columbus High band practiced marching and the football team scrimmaged. It was a fresh clear afternoon, a pleasant day for exploring. Suddenly Mat glimpsed a figure about a block away, spun his bike and rode furiously. I pedaled in pursuit, but by the time I caught up he had thrown his bike down and run over to his adversary. I was horrified to see how much bigger the boy was—three or four inches taller and forty pounds heavier.

Whatever words passed between them were over by the time I arrived.

There was no fear in the big boy's eyes, his expression held only contempt. Doubtless he thought Mat a fool. As I kept my distance, he reached out and shoved Mat away.

Mat hit him hard in the face. Startled, the boy gasped and cursed. He swung out furiously, but not before three more sharp jabs hammered his nose, his jaw and eyes. Dazed, the boy tried to throw his arms around his attacker, but Mat ducked under and pounded his stomach. Spitting and cursing, the boy blundered backward and forward, trying to find some defense. His look of disbelief and shock quickly evolved into one of fear. Mat was faster than I ever would have guessed. I don't believe the bully landed a single blow. He spun to turn his face away and Mat hit him on the back of the head. He fell to the ground and Mat's foot drove his face into the dirt. He scrambled away and when he finally found his footing he leaped up and ran.

My heart beating furiously, I watched my brother walk calmly to his bike, mount and ride off. He said nothing to me. There was not a scratch on him. I had been afraid he was about to get himself knocked crazy, now I shuddered at the intensity with which he had exacted his vengeance.

Within another month Mat had cornered the other two boys and given them a similar beating. I witnessed neither, but gathered that forewarned though they were, they simply could not reckon with the grim fearlessness of an enemy whose unthreatening stature demanded only scorn. To our knowledge, none of the three ever showed his face around Wynnton School again.

I wanted to talk to my brother about this, to understand, but he shut me up. "You keep quiet, Skeeter. What I do is nobody's business."

I hated to see him reduce everything to an animal level. I was afraid for the kind of boys he ran with, too, blasphemous, rebellious, profane. Mat's willingness, his eagerness even, to take every dare scared me.

And I knew he hated me. The summer he started driving he had to drop me off downtown. I was in the backseat, we were engaged in an argument and just as I opened the door to get out I said something spiteful. He slammed down on the accelerator so furiously that I had to stiffen my body and suck in my breath to keep from getting hit. When I got home I ran to my parents and told them how Mat had tried to kill me. He denied it, of course, but a month later I heard him telling some boys, "I tried to run over Skeeter once."

Strangely enough, he wouldn't let anyone else touch me. Maybe he was saving me for his personal kill. I felt safe under his protection and, as younger brothers do, looked up to him and desired his approval. But I still believed he hated me.

* * *

On Monday morning Miss Jenny Dean Barton marched into our Wynnton School classroom and in her bold, strong script wrote on the chalkboard, *An ounce of prevention is worth a pound of cure.* These proverbs were her first day of the week ritual. *Haste makes waste. A bird in the hand is worth two in the bush.* We were required to use the sayings in practicing our writing skills and to incorporate them into our daily lives. It was her way of imparting little gems of wisdom and words of caution. *Look before you leap. Don't count your chickens before they hatch.* By the end of the school year even the laggards among us had these ingrained words of wisdom.

Miss Barton wore stockings and carried a leather-strapped shoulder bag. Her hair was short, her words were clipped as with a paper cutter, her glance drilled right into our brains. She wore low-heeled walking shoes and long skirts. Her sharp nose and sculptured features gave her a stern yet wise look. We thought her mind was as quick as a steel trap. Whenever she gave us a drawing assignment she handed out gray poster paper. Always gray.

In her love for the English language, Miss Barton tolerated no slovenliness. When a girl raised her hand to ask, "Miss Barton, may I go and lay down? My head hurts," she cried, "What! Lay *what* down! Your legs? Your torso? It's *lie* down! Lie! You want to *lie* down!"

A day or two later some boy, trying to get it right, said, "Did you see Trudi? How does she get by with lying her head on the desk all the time?"

"No, no!" Miss Barton exclaimed. "She *lays* her head down. You *lie* down. You *lay* an object down. Please, please, please," she insisted, "learn when to use 'lie' and 'lay.' Learn when to use 'I' and 'me.' Before you leave this class you're going to learn how to speak correctly."

She hated the tacked on "at," too. "Where are you at? Tell them you're hiding behind the *at*!"

Often she got in her little points of chivalry. Gentlemen open doors for ladies. Gentlemen never walk ahead of ladies. And of character: Do what you say you will do. Keep your word. Take responsibility. *He that has an ill name is half hanged.*

The happiest moments of our rigid day came after big recess or lunch when Miss Barton read to us, most notably a chapter from *The Adventures of Remi*, by Hector Malot. Books were her friends, her consolation, and perhaps most of all she loved instilling appreciation for literature in young minds. Once she wrote a poem dedicated to one of her special pupils:

I have something to tell you, my dears,
Something your lives will bless.
A thing that will mean far more to you
Than money or fame or success
Is the power to enjoy the world's great books,
And to live through them, page by page,
Till it seems very real and not strange at all
To live in another age.
Old dead-eye Dick with his rollicking songs,
Robin Hood with his merry young thieves,
Will burst into life in these dearly loved books
By simply turning their leaves.
A land of enchantment is waiting for you!
By so simple and easy a trick

You'll be carried away to a strange new land.

Must I prove it! A story book, quick!

When she read to us, we envisioned her far removed from the class-room, traveling the dusty roads of *Remi* or climbing a hill to a nunnery on a far-off continent. Even the most fidgety among us were transformed into a part of the spellbound audience, absorbed by her clipped, Anglophilian expressions and devotion to good writing.

When Jenny Dean Barton swept into our steam-heated classroom with its pockets of chilly air, threw off her coat and dropped her books and papers onto the desk, then marched to the chalkboard to write her weekly proverb, some bolder boy would quip under his breath, "Our drill sergeant." One day when returning to class from lunch I extended my arms out like bird's wings, preventing those behind from passing. I didn't know the teacher had entered the room, but as soon as we sat down she looked directly at me and demanded an explanation. "What were you doing, Skeeter?"

I dropped my head and didn't speak.

"If you have no answer say, 'I don't know.'"

I sank lower into my desk and clamped my mouth tighter.

"Say, 'I don't know'!"

Finally I uttered the pointless words.

Her tone cold, she persisted, "If I ask you a question and you don't have an answer say, 'I don't know.' Do you understand?"

I nodded.

"Do you understand?"

"Yes, ma'am."

"Very well. Keep your arms at your side."

So Miss Barton was another of my fears. I understood that she was wise, and deep down I didn't believe her heart was so hard. I wondered if she could possibly tell me what would happen if my daddy lost his job, how long I would have to fear the evil old garage, and if I would ever have a new bike. If I asked her she would probably warn me against fearing things that might never occur.

Don't cross a bridge before you come to it.

* * *

Around two o'clock, school let out and there was a wild exodus across Wynnton's wide green lawn, some students running to cars lined up along the long curved driveway. I reached home in a matter of minutes. Before heading back up to the school to collect my newspapers, I had barely enough time to eat my usual peanut butter and banana sandwich and do some of my homework. Some of the neighborhood kids were already out on the street playing ball, but I had to work.

Back at the school I folded my papers, stacked them in my canvas bag, strapped the bag to my handlebars, and was off within ten or fifteen minutes after the *Ledger* truck dropped off the bundles. As I rode rapidly I extracted papers from the bag and sent them skidding without slackening my speed. This rhythm of pedaling, throwing, pedaling, throwing was a skill from which I derived some pride. I worked hard to try to be better and faster than any of the other boys.

The original Wynnton was a jewel on the trading town's breast, and as I rode the streets and avenues delivering papers or exploring I came across what was left of the great estates with landscaped grounds, gardens, orchards, servant houses, carriage houses, stables; multi-gabled mansions and stately columned porches and wrought-iron garden fences. Most of the big estates had been reduced to an acre or two surrounded by modest lots and houses. Even the mansion of Mr. William L. Wynn at the top of Wynn's Hill, the man for whom my school Wynnton was named, had been converted into a club building with narrow patches of grass. We were a cross-section of personality and character and social bearing. We had the hardware salesmen, the mill workers, the barbers, the druggists, as well as the man of arts, the world traveler, the statesman, the inventor, the educator, the railman, the musician.

By the time my daddy was able to bring his family to our little brick house on Schaul, Wynnton had become a nondescript middle-class neighborhood on fifty-foot lots with dirt driveways. Sometimes as I rode along streets lined with oaks and sycamores I was filled with longing, with the fear that I might miss out on a glorious life, that the elements of romance and nostalgia in me would never realize fruition. Sometimes I stopped my bike at the top of a gently sloping hill and looked down the avenue of trees and dwellings with urgency close to tears. These were people, they had all the desires and fears known to man, they wanted to live, they wanted something beautiful to happen, they wanted to experience their aliveness. A tremendous force seemed to overwhelm me, sweeping me away. I felt that if I concentrated hard enough I could levitate myself into the highest trees. I would be weightless, vaporous yet humanly substantial. I cried out suddenly, shouting to the top of my lungs. It made no difference, anyone who should poke his head out would simply see a silly kid making unnecessary clamor out on the street. For a moment I felt an urge to stand my Schwinn and force my face into the hard bark of a tree, to see what I could drive in or out of my skull, to convert the power of the brain into painless maniacal physicalness. I jumped onto my bike and flew down the hill, arms lifted high, sucking wind into my ridiculous singing.

I was turning across a sidewalk when the front wheel of my bike dropped down crazily into a roadside ditch. The homeowner had raked his yard and what appeared to be level ground was in fact a ditch full of leaves. I went flying over the handlebars and hit the ground. My knee struck the bike and there was a biting pain. I swore, "Damn!" the only useful curse word in my vocabulary so far. I yanked the bike out of the ditch and tried to ride, but discovered that the left fork had been bent and the warped wheel dragged too badly to turn. I looked about, hoping that by some miracle help would appear. There was no one in sight. I began to pull and yank on the fork but couldn't budge it. I saw nothing to do but walk the mile home for some tools. There was a sick feeling in my stomach, but head bent, hands in pockets, I plowed back to Schaul Street.

I fetched a hammer from the garage and hiked back to my bike. The western sky was tinging to crimson, more than an hour had been lost, and my nerves were growing tighter. I needed to finish before dark—if I finished at all.

I drove vengeful blows to the bent fork with little success. Finally I yanked the bike over to a big oak, braced the front wheel against the tree, and employed the hammer for leverage to twist and bend the fork enough for the wheel to turn. At last I was able to ride again, struggling to balance on a wobbly and unstable front end.

As darkness fell, I threw my last paper and dragged home, my shoulders sagging. When Daddy came in from work he took one look at my face. "What's the matter, Skeeter?"

"My bike."

"Broken down again?"

"It's messed up pretty bad this time."

"Well, let's have a look."

We went out and rolled the bicycle into the garage. By locking the frame into his vice and using a long pipe for leverage he was able to draw the fork fairly straight. The front wheel still bumped and vibrated, but I tried riding around our grassed backyard and with quickly learned skills of balance I was able to maneuver fairly well.

"Do you think I'll ever be able to get a new bike?" I asked Daddy.

"I don't know, Skeeter. Maybe someday."

I knew he couldn't afford a new bike, but I felt so deprived I couldn't help myself. "If you had a good job I bet I could get a decent bike." I'd heard Mama say things like this to him and I hated it—yet I was doing the same.

"I guess any job is better than nothing," said Daddy.

I knew my father didn't have a lazy bone in him. He would never look for a handout or accept charity. He worked hard and put everything he made into the nurture and care of his family. But I wondered how much longer I could earn money without a dependable bicycle. Whenever I felt

I was close to having enough money to buy one, I needed shoes or a shirt, or there was something else that took a chunk of my savings. When I saw one of the better-off boys on a shiny Schwinn I wondered why it had to be that my father was always broke and couldn't even be certain he'd have a job next week or next month.

* * *

Mat was employed by a service station washing cars, changing oil, sandblasting sparkplugs. He worked weekends and on the afternoons when the station needed him following school. Often he came home late and the family ate without him because Daddy usually had to go out on his own night job. Mat was driving now, he needed money for gas and dating, and seldom did he offer to cough up cash for the family.

One night Mat's sweetheart Margaret Howell called. It was unusual for girls to phone boys, but Margaret was too rich to care. I took the call and when I told her Mat was still working she, in her sweetest tone, asked me to have him call her back. I made the cardinal sin of forgetting—a cardinal sin because telephone messages were important.

When Mat found out, probably through Margaret's pouting, he was furious. "What kind of dumb ox is it that can't remember a simple phone call?"

"You're the dumb ox, not me," I retorted.

"You're old enough to do something around here."

"Do something! When did you mow a lawn or take out the garbage? If it weren't for me our room would be a pigsty."

The argument heated up, one thing led to another, and Mat grew more furious. Without warning he reached out and popped me on the forehead. His fist was closed but he used his middle knuckles and the pain was sharp. I could feel my forehead puffing up and knew there was a big red splotch where he'd hit me. I began to wail, louder than necessary, for I wanted Mama or Daddy to hear me.

Mat stepped back, I think he surprised himself, and I thought I detected a faint glint of remorse in his eyes. But it was more than remorse that I was looking for. I wanted him to say he was sorry. But he would never apologize.

"Oh, stop acting like a baby," he spat.

I ran to our bedroom, slammed the door—as if this would keep him out—and threw myself down on the bed. I wasn't that hurt or humiliated. My pain was of a deeper nature. I wanted someone to comfort me. But what chafed me most was that Mat could get away with anything. Even if he decided to kill me.

* * *

Daddy arrived home from work, went to the lavatory, rolled up his sleeves and washed up. He had strong hands and short capable fingers, sturdy wrists and forearms wreathed with bristly black hair. His arms were dark and sun-burnished, pigmented as with mechanic's oil, his nails rough and stubby, nails which were cleaned roughly with a pen knife. As we sat down to eat, Mat emerged from his world long enough to dodge discussions on his unfortunate grades at school. The meal then became a silent one, until toward the end Daddy remarked offhandedly, "Some Army officers came into the store today. I don't know what they wanted."

Mama perked up at once. "You think they're on to something?"

"Monty was with them. He didn't seem concerned."

Joanie had just been diagnosed with a serious kidney infection, perhaps needing hospitalization, and every day Mama anguished over the pharmacy bills. I anguished, too. I was afraid something bad would happen to my baby sister, and I wanted to be her protector and guardian. It couldn't be a worse time for Daddy's job to be threatened. Hardware and paint was all he knew, and if he left Chattahoochee his prospects for another job were dismal.

"It's not your business," Mama said at last.

"What if they ask? Am I supposed to lie?"

She clamped her mouth shut but I felt what she was thinking. This was a struggle between truthfulness and self-survival, a position that was painful for her and for us. My parents hated dishonesty, but their children came first—their children who needed medicine, food, shoes, shelter. It had to be only through the most primitive maternal instincts that Mother insisted Daddy keep quiet about this fraud at Chattahoochee Paint and hang onto his job under any circumstances.

"I wish I *didn't* know." Daddy ended the discussion, but I felt my stomach twist. I knew this burden weighed so heavily upon them that there was little room to lighten the atmosphere around the house.

After dinner I followed Daddy out to the garage, a building cluttered with shelves of tools and paint, old lawn chairs, motors, pulleys and cables and various sorts of blades. Daddy was a fixer and made use of everything. Growing up on a farm had taught him how to invent alternative repairs when parts were too expensive or unavailable, and never to throw anything away.

During his private work when no one was around he would steal a nip from a secret bottle he kept well concealed—just a nip, no more, for Mama was furiously opposed to alcohol. Many times she commissioned Mat and me to search the garage during his absence, but we never could uncover his hidden cache. Once I happened to discover him climbing down from the rafters, but by the time I could drag a ladder over the next day and search, no evidence of guilt could be found. He remained one step ahead of us, slipping into the garage at night and emerging chewing Clorets.

"You shouldn't drink, Daddy," I admonished him. "It's bad for you."

"What makes you think I drink?"

"You know from church you're supposed to keep your temple holy."

He grinned sheepishly. "Think about it as holy water."

I didn't believe Daddy would ever drink outside the seclusion of his garage or go anywhere with alcohol on his breath, but to push a point I said, "You don't want to give Mr. Montgomery anything to hold against you."

"I imagine Mr. Montgomery has whole shelves lined with bottles." Then he looked at me soberly. "Some men hold their whiskey, Skeeter, it makes a devil out of others. Don't you ever take a chance with it."

Though I was on Mother's side—I had witnessed a drunken uncle and it repulsed me—I wondered if Daddy's little nipping was a way to escape life's woes. I understood why he might resort to most anything that offered a short-lived reprieve. Not only was his badly needed job in jeopardy, his integrity was in jeopardy. The threat of being implicated in fraud weighed as heavily on him as the dread of seeing his family suffer.

"I wish I didn't know." He said it again and again.

* * *

Daddy was reared on a small Alabama farm, rode his little Shetland pony five miles to school in the worst weather, emigrated to Columbus at an early age, and learned a smattering of grammar and math at the old Industrial High. He landed a job at William Beach Hardware on Broadway, first riding his bicycle to deliver small orders and collect accounts, but in time moved into the store as a salesman. During World War II all commodities were in short supply, and he worked with the requisition officers at Ft. Benning, Georgia, to find scarce items. It was said that if Nathan Harding couldn't find a thing it couldn't be found.

Columbus was founded as a port town and in its early days paddle-wheelers and steam barges chugged up and down the Chattahoochee energizing the cotton trade. By the time Daddy arrived it had established some reputable credentials. It was the birthplace of Coca-Cola. It was the site of the last battle of the Civil War. It was where the first idea for a national Memorial Day was spawned (though we all knew half a dozen states would challenge us on this). It was a place where travelers could leave their hotel rooms unlocked, their car windows down, packages on the seats, and the Lord's Prayer and the Pledge of Allegiance were recited every morning in classrooms.

When Daddy left William Beach for a better paying job at Chatta-hoochee Paint and Hardware, he had no warning of the mistake he'd made. He was a hardworking man, always willing to give a good day's work for a day's pay, never expecting a handout, and doing everything within his physical and intellectual capabilities to support his wife and three children. With the war over and young men and women being repatriated back to the States the work force became greater than the demand, jobs, especially on the skill level of Daddy's, were hard to find, and he was torn between the tension of absolute honesty and feeding his family.

Daddy by nature was a cheerful person, undeniably responsible for his wife and children, honest to a fault. He hardly knew how to mount defenses against an assault on his character and possibly going to jail.

So we watched him trudge off each morning with a slight drag to his feet, a slight slump to his shoulders, a firm determination to his fine lips, not knowing if he would return home at night a man with a job and salary or one who if worse came to worst could find his family thrown out of its home.

Nevertheless, when he went out after supper to work in his small shop—he was never without some trifling project underway—his step was firm, his demeanor optimistic, his mouth twisted with some inaudible whistle.

* * *

I left Daddy in the garage and went in to play with Joanie a few minutes before she went to bed. She was a mama's girl but she loved me and was as likely to climb into my lap as Mama's when she wanted attention. Her hair was the color of vanilla caramel, her eyes blue, her cheeks high like Mother's, and she could spend hours amusing herself.

After Joanie went to bed I walked out onto our front porch. Our house was never cool. In summer air was drawn in by one large window fan, and it was never warm but heated by two small space heaters, one in the bathroom, the other in the living room. There was a front grassed yard elevated on a low terrace, and a large rear yard which we mowed with a reel plush mower.

Next to us was a vacant lot where Spanish Bayonet grew, affording the neighborhood children an extravagance of swords with which to fight our enemies. These spears with sharp edges and pointed tips we handled with respect, knowing that used carelessly they could cause painful injury. There were no sidewalks, the grass ran right down to the curb, and clotheslines strung across backyards were fair identification of the breadwinner's vocation: dungarees, overalls, underwear, heavy flannel or starched white shirts.

The town had been founded in 1827 as a trading post on the site of an old Indian village along the Chattahoochee River, and it became the South's first industrial center. During the Civil War shoes and swords were made for the soldiers, and there was a shipyard for the Confederate Army. Along the river were great grist and textile mills. On Tenth Avenue was Lummus Gin Company which manufactured cotton gins shipped everywhere, and on Front Street were the massive warehouses to whose docks farmers were led by puffs of cotton which blew off trucks like restless white pigeons. On Tenth, too, was Tom Houston Peanut Company, whose tantalizing odors of boiling peanuts, molasses, and candy could be detected all around town.

Most of the houses on Schaul had porches, some large and wide across entire fronts and supported by heavy round wood columns or ornamental iron, others small but almost always spacious enough for a couple of iron chairs or a swing. It wasn't unusual to see several people from up and down the street on one porch, then half an hour later see the same people on another porch. No one ever locked their doors and if my mother happened to need a stick of butter she didn't hesitate to let herself into the kitchen of our neighbors, the Parises, to borrow one. I was just as likely to come home and find Mrs. Paris rummaging through our cabinets in search of something she needed.

The Parises had two daughters a little younger than I, and were in the building supply business. Lovely Leigh Ann Minor lived next to them with her retired Air Force father and her career specialist mother. Jean Gresham lived across and up the street, with her mother and grandmother, and on the opposite end were the Quinceys who had holdings in real estate and fought so hard they finally had to divorce. Mr. Quincey, a raconteur of an inexhaustible sort, had a million words in his repertoire, and would stand talking through a neighbor's screen door on dozens of subjects. "I wish as a young man I had learned to take life less seriously," Mr. Quincey would say, but he was dead serious about his fractious relations with his ex-wife. Mostly everyone liked Mr. Quincey, though when they saw him ambling up the street they hid behind drawn curtains.

On the corner of Henry and Schaul were my friend Malcolm Hughley and his family. Mr. Hughley drove a delivery truck and kept a Bible on the seat beside him. Across from them were the Rileys, whose mentally challenged son was a kleptomaniac who picked up anything that didn't belong to him, causing his parents misery. And finally, there was old Miss Jones who lived in the biggest house on the street, a real mausoleum, and who pinched pennies to the point that she practically starved herself.

Altogether it wasn't much to boast about, but it was ours. Of all the thousands of houses around us in all the neighborhoods like Wynnton and St. Elmo and Overlook we could travel anywhere and return like honeybees to our little bungalows on Schaul Street. As Miss Barton said, *A bird likes its own nest.* But probably every one of us wanted to leave Schaul, we wanted bigger houses, we needed more money and a better life.

I doubted that very many adults realized how much a ten-year-old understands. I had a business, earned and saved money, had my own shoes resoled, bought presents for my family. I read the paper, had a good grasp of math, felt sadness, fear, longing, wondered about God, planned to grow up and find a well-paying job. But a child is compelled to remain silent, hardly ever invited to share his wisdom. Our grasp of things was much greater that most adults realized but we were trapped in in the obedience of childhood.

As the cold of the concrete steps began to seep through me, the dread I felt was not of the night chill. It was something more bizarre and more ominous, a straining forward for something I couldn't identify, a fear of what might lurk around the next dark corner.

3

My wobbly front wheel forced me to develop a certain finesse of balance. Still, I frequently came perilously close to crashing into trees or dropping off curbs. Mat had a bike, a good one, vintage Schwinn, better than mine. While he was driving now and might look with some disdain on a poor cyclist, he still had to rely on his bicycle when the car wasn't available. He had treated it roughly, slamming it around when it became victim of his anger. I wasn't sure I wanted to appropriate it even if he would let me. It needed a good overhaul but the only thing I could think of was a new bike, and I needed it so badly that as Christmas approached I schemed to pick up some extra cash. I bought a hundred twenty cheap Christmas cards, and over a couple of weeks I knocked on almost every door of my route, handed my customer a card and said, "I just wanted to wish you a merry Christmas." The response was usually a hesitant "Just a minute," then the customer would disappear and come back with a handful of change or maybe a dollar bill, and once or twice a five. It was shamefully akin to begging. I felt a tinge of guilt. But on the positive side, I was able to stuff a significant number of extra bills into the secret cigar box on the floor of my closet.

We held our breath, though, as Daddy went to work every morning not knowing if he would return home unemployed. "Mr. Montgomery wouldn't fire someone right at Christmas, would he?" I asked Mama anxiously.

"That man's capable of anything," she said. "But the store's really busy at this time of year, I doubt that he'll be letting anybody go."

Despite my worry I joined in the excitement at Wynnton School during the Christmas season. We all wrote our names on slips of paper and deposited them into a basket. As the teacher walked the aisles each of us reached into the basket to draw a slip. Mine was for a boy named Andrew Salt. It was agreed that no one would divulge whose names we drew, and since I didn't know Andrew that well all I could hope was that he'd like the same things I liked. After some consideration I bought a small telescope with which to conduct spying operations. I wrapped this and hoped he'd be thrilled to receive it.

Not until the day of the exchange did I learn that our teacher had drawn my name. This was when the class scrambled to pass out gifts and tear away ribbons and wrappings. Miss Barton came down the aisle, placed her present on my desk, and warned, "Don't you dare open this, Skeeter, until your parents see it."

Her reason was evident. She must have spent hours wrapping the gift. On gleaming white slick paper she had pasted balloon-like circles of poster paper in various sizes and colors. Every perfectly arranged cutout of the beautiful wrappings had to be testimony of tender feelings toward its contents. This was the first time I'd ever seen her use anything but gray, and both her pride in her handiwork and her recognition of my parents' appreciation surprised me. While the other kids tore into their gifts I impatiently waited, and as soon as school was over I ran home clutching Miss Barton's present under my arm. The suspense wasn't over yet. I promised her I'd wait until my parents admired the wrappings before tearing them away and Daddy wouldn't be home for hours. It was only after I'd thrown my newspapers and the afternoon had dragged by that I was able to show them my present.

"Miss Barton drew my name, and she wanted you to see this before I open it."

"It's especially pretty," Mama said.

"Lots of work just to be ripped apart," said Daddy.

Joanie, wide-eyed, ran her fingers gently over the paper, touching each bright circle. "Bawoon," she whispered.

At last I tore into the paper and found one of Miss Barton's favorite of all books, *The Adventures of Remi*. Pasted to the inside cover were photographs of her and her sister in various parts of Europe where scenes of *Remi* had taken place. Though I might have yearned for something more useful, like a Boy Scout canteen or B-B's for my Daisy, it did occur to me that in me Miss Barton had perhaps seen something of promise, and in this respect I felt special and puffed up for several days.

* * *

When Miss Barton looked at me with her drilling eyes and said sternly, "I do believe you can do better, Skeeter," or "Is *this* the paper you wish to turn in?" it drove fear straight into my heart. "Your papers could be better organized, Skeeter, but I do believe your script is improving." The care and thoughtfulness with which she presented me *The Adventures of Remi* implied a degree of respect, though it's quite possible I mistook this for her love for the book. At least I could flatter myself by believing she would never have gone to such lengths to decorate the gift for a pupil in whom she had little confidence.

One cold morning when we were all walking back to the classroom from the playground something shining caught my eye. I ran over and discovered several coins which evidently had fallen from someone's pocket. I scooped them up, three quarters, two dimes, several nickels, and half a dozen pennies. How fortunate I was! I had to work hard for every cent I earned, and such a windfall sent a thrill of excitement through my chilled bones. But before I slipped the coins into my pocket I looked around to see if anyone appeared to be searching. I would of course give them back could I find the rightful owner, though I knew that in Wynnton were quite a few students who could lose a pocketful of change and never miss it.

Then I noticed Jack our janitor watching me from a few feet away, and I realized what had happened. Jack had spied the money about the same time as I and was hastening to it when I cut him off. I could see the letdown in his face. He made no effort to challenge me, simply stood motionless.

We all knew Jack only by his first name. He was a strong black man upon whom staff and teachers depended for everything. Where he lived and his family circumstances were unknown to us. With the children, the janitor was neither condescending nor withdrawn. The scathing rebuke of Jack was dreaded almost as much as that of a teacher. He would sternly call us down about doing anything wrong or dangerous, recognizing neither wealth nor class, but only his responsibility to keep us safe. A pretty little rich girl earned the janitor's admonition just as quickly as did her poor classmate. He remained indispensable, unobtrusive and in a strange way sad, called on in emergencies, mopping up vomit and firing the basement furnaces on cold mornings so the classrooms would be warm when students arrived.

Jack had missed the money. I was a step ahead of him, and I imagined that all the visions of what he might do with it flew by like blue jays vanishing into the trees. Having scarcely paused, he averted his gaze and turned to resume his journey across the grounds.

I held out my hand, stopping him. "Here, Jack." The coins still glistened brightly in my palm. Instinctively he turned his hand up and I dropped them in. He gazed at them solemnly. We both knew the right thing to do was turn the money in to the school's lost and found. Some hapless pupil might yet be looking for it. But seeing his need and his hesitation I said, "Keep it, Jack."

He didn't smile, hardly acknowledged the gesture at all. In some unexplained way my sanction granted him license to accept something which belonged to neither of us. He nodded and continued on across the yard, hand in pocket, fingering the coins, and I hurried to class.

A few days later I was freezing against a pillar of the outdoor corridor

31

and dreading the long afternoon on my paper route. It was miserably cold. I was sensitive to cold anyway, and my coat wasn't the warmest. The canyon between the main school building and the cafeteria invited the blasts of a whipping north wind. Students were prohibited from entering the classrooms during recess and lunch, and I had sought the meager protection of a column when I felt a tug on my sleeve and turned to see Jack standing next to me. He said nothing, just motioned me to follow. We went through the heavy double doors which led down through a sooty concrete stairway into the basement.

This was off limits to the students. Whenever we tried to slip through the doors to get a break from the cold we were thoroughly chastised. At the bottom of the stairs was the furnace room holding coal, shovels, buckets, mops, cleaning equipment, and all the tools janitors require to maintain a school building. It was grimy and possibly dangerous. But on bitterly cold days, scant minutes on the upper dark stairway landing could provide luxuriant warmth to chilled bones. This was where Jack took me.

"Jack, are you sure you won't get in trouble?" I asked.

"Naw. It's all right."

At the foot of the blackened stairs the furnaces glowed cheerfully. The odors of coal, oils, lubricants and soap and sweat wafted up in caustic drifts. I did not want to touch anything with my clothes. I felt that coal soot was everywhere. But the radiant heat—this meant everything. I breathed it into my skin, through my jacket and into my chest which moments before had turned cold draughts into exhaled ghostly vapors.

"You stay on the steps here, now," said Jack.

"I will, Jack. And thank you."

For the months of cold weather this became a ritual. Jack would find me standing outside in the cold, teeth chattering, and spirit me into the forbidden furnace room. "C'mon in here now. Hurry. Don't let nobody see."

He went ahead, paused, looked around, then as I slipped over quickly he held the heavy doors open.

"Anybody watching, Jack?"

"Naw. But it never hurts to look before you leap."

I had never considered whether Jack paid attention to what was written on Miss Barton's chalkboard, but I knew this came straight from it.

I enjoyed the intrigue as much as the warmth itself, and I became the grudging envy of the few classmates who caught wind of my special privilege. Though there was hardly a word that passed between us I was aware of Jack's presence. I had been kind to him, and he was repaying my kindness. The gift comes back to the giver, I'd heard a pastor say. I felt that if I needed Jack he would hurry to my rescue. I wished I could do something for him. But I was a boy and he was a grown man. I wished that he could accompany me to the dreadful garage on Henry Avenue. I didn't have the courage to tell him about my fears.

* * *

How Miss Barton could have known of my compact with Jack I couldn't imagine, but I felt that somehow she did know. Following the incident with the lost coins she seemed to treat me more kindly. But most of us still thought of her as a cold fish.

Then one morning I saw a soft side of Miss Barton. At the end of Wynnton's exterior corridors were heavy ornamental iron gates. These were opened early by the janitor, and closed and locked when school was over. Every student knew to keep his hands off these swinging gates once they had been opened and held fast by small brackets attached to the wall.

On that morning several mischievous fourth graders decided to release the gates and swing them shut against a fellow pupil emerging from a car on the street. In their haste one of the boys left his hand in the wrong place, and the closing gates all but severed his second finger.

I happened to be close by, and when he let out a blood-curdling yell I ran over to see what was going on. The boy stood petrified, staring at his finger which had been so nearly cut off the joint hung by a thread. It was a ghastly sight, and I felt a sweeping sickness in my stomach. The boy did not move, just stood crying hysterically as blood oozed down his arm and into his coat sleeve. Someone ran to the school office, but the rest of us stood in mute horror.

Miss Barton was first to arrive. When she saw the hand her face went white. She opened her mouth in a gasp, then set her jaw and swept the children aside. "Out of the way!" She put her arm around the boy's shoulder. "It's all right, now. It's all right, Clarence. Walk with me. Come on, I've got you."

She spoke continuously, in a hushed voice, "It's all right now. You'll be fine. We'll just get you to the office..." Little spatters of blood fell along the corridor all the way. In seconds they disappeared into the office, and a few minutes later a car sped away taking him to the hospital.

All morning pupils kept asking, "Did you see his finger? It was nearly cut off."

"I have a cousin who lost the end of his finger. You can get along without it."

"But it'll be so...freakish!"

I thought of the horrible sight and turned a little sick again.

During the afternoon we learned that the surgeons had been able to reattach the finger, but just barely. Almost immediately, our principal, Mr. Buxton, whom no one dare cross, sent out an edict that any student caught fooling with the iron gates would be expelled. But for me and some others the real drama was Miss Barton.

"I'm sorry to find out her heart's not stone," one boy said. "Now I don't have to hate her when she makes me write, 'I will not go to sleep in class' a hundred times."

Not waiting for her usual Monday morning ritual, Miss Barton re-covered, went to the blackboard that afternoon and wrote a new proverb: *Haste makes waste*, one which I sensed would serve as apt advice to us in the future.

All afternoon and evening I couldn't get my mind off Clarence. My flesh crawled when I thought it could have happened to me. When finally all my papers were delivered, the evening was over and I fell into bed, I lay awake listening to the toots and coupling of railcars on the yard three miles away.

I wondered where the trains were going, how many tunnels, bridges, and valleys would be presented to the wandering eye, what sleepy little towns would be passed through. I wondered about the children running along with the train, the shacks, the mansions, but mostly about the people doing their daily tasks. I turned over and scrunched down my pillow, the longing of my spirit like an iron gate closing on my thoughts.

* * *

On Saturday morning I rode my bike to town and decided to swing by Linwood Cemetery, turn up through the entrance and drift down the paths, reading the headstones. I liked old houses, old barns, old cemeteries and churchyards. Why, I didn't know. Perhaps because of the wonderful classic stories Miss Barton read to us. In fifth grade I had a job, pretty much made my own way, assumed responsibility and sometimes felt much older than other ten-year-olds. Here in Linwood I imagined the lives of those earlier pioneers, heard cowbells and smelled grain fields, fought a soldier's battle and listened to a mother whispering to her child, a father reading to his family by candlelight. All around me were old cedar trees, crepe myrtle and dogwood and Nandina bushes, with markers of every size — tall spear-pointed spires, pyramids, obelisks, all formed from granite, marble, or concrete. Ornamental iron fences enclosed some of the family plots, and there were splashes of artificial and real flowers.

An upright rectangular marker was inscribed, "Joseph Leary, 1827-1859," and beneath, "A Strong Man in Deed and Spirit." This man had died at just thirty-two, much younger than my father, and I stood, straddling my bike, wondering what sort of life he led, if he were a merchant or farmer, a cotton factor or teacher, if he had children, what his house was like. Mostly, I imagined people much like myself, reaching for something lively and grand, seeking what I supposed must have been called a romantic life, robust, vibrant, breathing clear blue air. By living vicariously in the experiences of others I escaped for a moment from my own fears and uncertainties.

In a lower section of Linwood was a quadrant memorializing the Confederate dead. I leaned my bike against a tree and walked through, thinking of the courage and love of the men behind the names. "1st Sgt. Benjamin Fuller, Co. G, 7 Florida Infantry, CSA, June 17, 1862, Age 18." Eighteen, just two years older than my brother. Through some strange quirk this soldier out of the past assumed my brother's face, and I quickly jumped onto my bike and pedaled away. It was a horrible war, brother against brother, but whether farmer or soldier, people died young in those days and all I could think of was that most had to work so hard they had little time to make their dreams come true. Somehow, though, thoughts of another time, another life, appealed to the romantic side of me.

I rode out of Linwood and detoured down to the river on the way to the *Ledger* to pay my bill. In an almost perfect grid, the streets were laid out running east and west, avenues north and south. In the median dividing Broadway were well-spaced trees where thousands of birds roosted. Doves and hummingbirds found the environment favorable in summer, and a few ducks swam on the backwaters in winter. Downtown were all the original churches, Baptist, Methodist, Presbyterian, Catholic, with their great spires and belfries and bell towers. On Saturdays I sometimes would buy a bag of peanuts from one of the vendors who were sitting on the wall in front of the Post Office, selling homemade soap and crafts, bags of peas, sugarcane, syrup, sage brooms, candles, small bundles of kindling.

The bridges interested me most. Their histories dated from the eighteen-hundreds, when a black slave named Horace King became a master bridge builder. He was less a slave than a partner with his master John Godwin, who educated him, gave him his freedom and set King on the path to great success. It intrigued me that this man could so spectacularly rise above his circumstances to become an engineer and builder sought by counties throughout the south to construct bridges and structures following his own innovative designs. The original wood-covered bridges were before my time, but King's work lived on as an inspiration to black and white alike.

The original trading post was established on a bluff overlooking the Chattahoochee and named after Christopher Columbus, probably influenced by the writings of Washington Irving. The headwaters of the Chattahoochee began in north Georgia, not much more than a small stream, but by the time it traversed the banks through Atlanta and on to Columbus, demarking the Georgia-Alabama state lines, it had become a significant river. From time to time the two states engaged in a fruitless argument as to where their state boundaries really were, but we in Columbus knew the Chattahoochee belonged to us up to the high water mark on the Alabama side. All up and down both riverbanks could be found old Indian burial mounds and artifacts and relics dating back, according to the geologists, millions of years.

Out on the Fourteenth Street Bridge, I watched the current as it whipped against the pilasters. The water was red from upstream erosion, and river bottom sedimentation had pretty much halted the paddle-wheelers which had chugged upriver in the old days, transporting bales of cotton. I remembered a story my grandmother had told me. I didn't know if she'd been a witness or had simply heard about it. In a torrential upriver rain one of Horace King's wooden bridges spanning the Georgia/Alabama banks at Columbus had been torn loose from its moorings and floated majestically, intact, downstream until it was caught up on a bower of trees. When the waters receded, determined Columbusites brought their mules and barges and tow lines down river and floated the bridge back upstream to its anchorage. It was said that a bunch of Huckleberry-Finn-type Alabama boys jumped onto the bridge and rode it upstream, shouting out turns and snags and sandbars, but I had an idea there was no truth in this part of the story.

On several corners along Broadway were old horse and dog waterers.

At one time farmers and landowners could bring their mule wagons and carriages into town for supplies and water their horses and dogs at the iron water pots. These were long gone, but I missed them as I missed the old streetcar tracks that had been ripped out and paved over. Probably what I enjoyed most was not the long shaft which rose from the trolleys to the wires above, hissing and spitting like bumper cars, but the clanging of the bells as they pulled into the transfer station on Twelfth and Broad.

One landmark that had not disappeared, and never would I hoped, was at the intersection of Wynnton and Buena Vista Roads where I passed almost every time I came to town. It was a large fountain and statue of a lady leaning forward like the prow of a ship, her arm raised to shield her eyes, looking toward some distant unknown object or happening, in a state of perpetual expectancy. It was made of white marble and since so many Columbus girls married Ft. Benning soldiers the statue was fondly called, "A Columbus mother looking for a son-in-law...." In truth, it was a fountain-statue dedicated to the memory of Mrs. Leonora Starling, who died in an automobile wreck in 1928.

I traveled the streets listening to ribbons of music from too-loud radios, inhaling the delicious odors of peanuts and candy from Tom Houston, and wondering if I might ever become more than a tiny speck on this wondrous throbbing globe.

4

My friend Tommy and I were sitting in my tent, my most prized possession. I'd received it a Christmas ago, much to my surprise because I knew my parents couldn't afford it. The canvas was heavy and strong, waterproof, and it was large enough for three sleeping bags.

Tommy sat in the grass with his arms around his knees, and I had my legs stretched straight out. "If we have to move," I said, "I wonder if I'll be able to take my tent with me."

"Why would you move?" asked Tommy.

"My daddy might lose his job."

"Cripes, that's the pits. What's happened?"

I couldn't tell him the reason, of course. "I just mean if the store closed or something. Have you ever wondered what you'd do if you got thrown out of your house?"

"It'd never happen," said Tommy. "My dad works for the government." Then he must have noticed my glum expression. With a tone of excitement he said, "Hey, I've got an idea. Why don't we camp out tonight? Tomorrow's Saturday. And look at this weather. It's like Spring."

Camping out was usually a summertime event. We would pitch the tent in various locations around our backyard or against the rear wall of our garage. There was no floor, the grass was our mattress and in winter the ground was usually too cold, the turf like brittle spears beneath the sleeping bags.

I jumped at the idea. "Who else could we invite?"

"Charlie, maybe, and T-Tom."

Neither Charlie nor T-Tom ran in our neighborhood, but we had ulterior motives. We knew that if some marauding threat came upon us during the night, Charlie would be first up, teeth bared and fists clenched, to confront the danger. Charlie was from a poor family with a multitude of misfit kin. He alternated about three changes of clothing, wore the same pants a week at a time, and kicked around in hand-me-down shoes which were too big for his feet. He cursed with pleasure, had bad teeth and endured little discipline from a house full of cousins and in-laws.

T-Tom's family was better off. He often had money in his pocket and shared sodas and banana splits. He was a tough, scrappy, thickly built boy who kicked off his shoes and socks to prowl the neighborhood barefoot.

Both Charlie and T-Tom jumped at the opportunity. Realizing Charlie probably couldn't scrounge up money for food and Sterno, I eased his mind. "I've got stuff to eat, Charlie. You don't need to bring anything."

"I can get something."

"Don't worry about it. Bring matches, though. We'll light candles."

Charlie was from a family of misfits, cousins and unkempt uncles and siblings, poorer than we. Whereas my daddy would never want or accept a handout, Charlie's clan reveled in them, and he himself had been recipient of a gift I envied. Some benevolent soul had had a bicycle refurbished and upgraded and painted, and given it to Charlie, who protected it as though it were his only soulmate. It was a great rebuild, some master technician had taken great care, added some innovations with sprockets and brakes, and finished with an artistic flourish—racing stripes and festoons. But then I shamed myself for envy, and was glad that Charlie at least had this one prized possession.

I cleared with Mama that we'd spend the night out in our backyard.

"Why do you like that tent so much?"

"I don't know. I guess it's sort of my place. Where I can be free."

"Free. I'm sure about breakfast time you'll be happy to come back to this prison."

Joanie, pulling her baby doll around in her wagon, said, "Me, too?"

"Oh, you want to spend the night in the tent?" I said.

She nodded her head vigorously.

I laughed. "No, this is a boy thing, Joanie. Besides, it's too cold for you."

She followed me outside when I went out to secure the tent, tighten the tie-downs and make certain the stakes were driven in firmly. These tasks I accomplished with excited motivation but also an element of distress. Our little house, our narrow backyard and peeling windows and junk-filled garage were nothing to boast about, but they were our shelter against storms, our refuge against danger. The possibility of losing our house made everything seem precious.

The boys arrived around six o'clock. Darkness was already creeping in, and to our surprise the balmy day ushered in an early evening chill. We drew our jackets tighter and started a fire in a shallow pit we'd dug, surrounded by two layers of brick. We dumped our beans and wieners into our frying pans and held them over the fire. The odors of frying food and crushed grass and honeysuckle vines made our stomachs growl, and we tried to eat while the food was too hot. The sky grew darker, the stars winked with half-caged eyes, windows that had been open earlier to the warm afternoon began to clatter closed, and we felt ourselves more and more isolated, as though not camping out in a narrow backyard surrounded by mostly silent houses, but in some remote wilderness.

"Getting cold," said T-Tom, who'd stripped off shoes and socks but now pulled them on again.

We huddled around the fire long after the glow faded, laughing, talking about everything that came to mind.

"I saw that new Frankenstein movie," said Tommy. "Weird."

"That Boris Karloff's got some horrible face."

"Aw, it's just the way he's made up. In real life he probably just looks normal."

We told ghost stories. "Blood on the first step…blood on the second step…"

T-Tom made the first move. "I'm getting my ass in my sleeping bag." We all crawled into our bags, zipping them up to our chins. Four were too many to spread out with any degree of comfort, but by pressing to the sides and making puzzle-like shapes we managed. In these distorted positions sleep was nearly impossible, but sleep wasn't what we had in mind. We continued our rambling dialogue until lights in the neighboring houses blinked out and sounds faded. Mat returned home from a date with his girlfriend Margaret, and nighttime closed over the town like the lid of a trunk.

Then Tommy said, "Let's go."

This would not be our first clandestine exploit. We liked to ramble, a small squadron on a secret mission, stalking the darkest shadows. Generally, it was innocent enough; the worst thing we had done was toss rocks at streetlights, shocked when one of us scored a hit. Once we discovered a small foreign car sitting on the curb next to two large oak trees. Taking hold of front and back we were able to wedge the little car directly between the trees, a terrible dilemma for the poor owner when he came out next morning to go to work. For this sin I paid with several weeks of shameful remorse. I knew I would always remember this meanness with regret.

With the anticipation of criminals about to make a heist we crawled out of our sleeping bags, vests and jackets pulled tight, and slipped out through our backyard in absolute silence. The back window of our bedroom, where Mat slept, was a darker shape against the dark-layered wall, but by now we knew it would take a bomb to rouse him. The mostly bare trees looked different against a shrouded moon, the limbs interwoven lines etched into pools of darkness. Skylight bathed the yards but not so brightly as to expose hastily concealed movement. Concealment was important. We needed to see without flashlights, to dodge through or jump over hedges, yet at the same time to be able to freeze against the hovering shadows of tree trunks, still as statues, as cars passed.

42

"We better walk," said T-Tom, "to keep my ass from freezing off."

"Your ass could stand some freezing off," said Charlie.

Not until we were well down the street and half a block away did we begin to talk and giggle again. A stealthy excitement vibrated through us, and even the air became electric. I realized that, frightened of the unknown as I was, with these accomplices I assumed an armored courage, a kind of delicious fearlessness, but there was something more—I must have possessed an element of criminality, of subterfuge and cunning which was so unlike my shy nature.

In the darkness we skulked north to Marion, thence on past Wynnton Road, up Eberhart and to Thirteenth Street. Our technique was unerring vigilance. We kept our eyes peeled for cars, and the moment we saw headlights we scrambled over hedges, behind trees. The headlights came on and on, flicking in the branches, sweeping the asphalt like liquid brooms as we crouched or stood stiffly, scarcely breathing. Usually it was not a police car but merely someone heading to or from night work, or a teenager without curfew.

At the wide intersections of Thirteenth we stood listening and looking a long time before sprinting across the open expanse like Army patrols charging under moonlight. Our greatest risk was stealing up through the business section which ran for blocks, continuous walls and fronts of store buildings with few alleys in which to hide, and no trees. Here we separated, Tommy and I on one side of the street, T-Tom and Charlie sidling up the opposite. Colonial Bakery was about halfway up Thirteenth and we knew bakers must be inside, for we inhaled the tantalizing odors of baking bread. The glass storefronts were mundane and undramatic by day, but intriguing and ghostly under muted moonlight.

I peered into a flower shop where chilled blooms and tiny ornaments—an arbor, an elfin bride and groom—and lacy, artificial leaves could be seen in an eerie backlight. Looking through the polished glass I felt myself transported into a moment of dream in which I wandered through a lush garden where I alone was master of the silence. I moved to the glass doors which presented a slightly different perspective. Absentmindedly, I turned the front door handle and to my amazement the door swung open. Evidently, the owner had forgotten to lock up! Shocked, I slammed the door and ran after Tommy, who had walked ahead. Of all the doors along the street, this happened to be the one I tried—I couldn't believe it!

"That door was open!" I exclaimed.

"What door?"

"The flower shop. I turned the handle and the door swung open."

No sooner had I reported this than from across the street Charlie shrieked, "Cops!"

I must have set off a silent alarm!

Tommy and I spun to look down Thirteenth. Headlights were bobbing through the intersection and coming up the hill fast. T-Tom and Charlie ran up onto the porch of a mortuary on their side of the street and froze in the shadows of the columns. Tommy and I were trapped in the open, without even a car to hide behind. At the last instant we ran *toward* the headlights to a shallow offset in a storefront wall. Tommy reached it first and flattened himself against the narrow space. I pressed hard against him, head down, squeezing him against the brick. I could just picture the cops picking us up, hauling us to town and telephoning my parents. "Mr. Harding, we have your son down here at headquarters. What's a ten-year-old doing roaming the streets at two in the morning?" I had been rebellious, I had been sassy, but never had I done anything to earn the disrespect of my parents. Now they would never trust me again, never allow me to sleep out in my tent or spend the night with another boy! And what if Mr. Montgomery heard about it? What better excuse to fire my father than that his ten-year-old roamed the streets at night! A python gripped my stomach.

But the cops didn't spot us, nor were they checking out the flower shop. We stood motionless another moment listening for the sound of braking and for the patrol cars to come back. But they went on, and Charlie and T-Tom ran across the street to join us. "Jesus, that was close," said Charlie. "They musta had a call."

"We better get out of here anyway," said T-Tom. "There could be others."

We all jumped when we heard a loud pop! pop! pop! about three blocks away.

"Damn!" cried Charlie. "Those must have been shots!"

"Gunshots? You sure?"

"I know a revolver when I hear one. Let's get the hell away from here!"

We took off running, then slowed to a steady trot once we were off Thirteenth. I thought about getting caught by the police, about the gunfire, and my parents waking to find I wasn't asleep in the tent. I should have known that the evil of the old garage could follow me anywhere anytime and wondered if this was a warning for me.

Our initial escape had been executed adroitly and rapidly, but our return was a painstaking journey, tense with caution. We spoke little and stole from shadow to shadow like burglars. At last we crept up our driveway single file to avoid blocs of movement, slid across the whispering grass and collapsed, with groans, into our sleeping bags. All anybody uttered was an occasional "Damn!" as we slithered between cold covers, so awkward that we kicked and head-butted one another.

By the time sleep descended upon us the eastern sky had already begun to glow, and way off in the distance a lonely dog awoke. We'd been on an adventure, come within a hair of getting caught by the police, stumbled close to gunfire, and by daylight we were paying for it. We stirred and rose with heavy leaded joints, muscles aching from the unnatural contortions with which we half slept. T-Tom, Tommy and Charlie rolled up their sleeping bags, and departed down our driveway in the pastel light, while I left all my stuff and skulked through our backdoor into the house. Mama was starting breakfast, and the comforting smells and sights of the warm kitchen bathed me in a sweet balm.

"Well, how was it?"

"Okay," I murmured.

"You look like something the dogs dragged in."

I splashed sleep from my eyes, feeling guilty for deceiving my parents, but it was deceit only to the extent that I had found out something about myself. I'd do it again if it meant throwing off my fear and fitting my heart and spirit with wings.

* * *

We decided it was too cold to think about sleeping out again, so a couple of the boys helped me repitch the tent against the back wall of our storage room where there was some protection from the wind. We dug a pit underneath to provide headroom, and I secreted a small treasure box containing some of my prized possessions on the ledge in one corner. Quite often I went out alone, sat on the cold earth and worried about Daddy losing his job, about Mat's temper, and about the old haunted garage. I thought about a new bike, too. It would be blue, with white racing stripes, a good chain guard...

Despite its ragged condition Mat had fitted his bike with narrow wheels, good for speed but not good for balance and traction through wet grass and muddy side yards. So I didn't ask him for it and doubted that he would give it up anyway. He may have had some sympathy for my plight, but I figured my wellbeing was just about at the bottom of his priorities. I suppose he felt toward me a sibling's protectiveness but devoted little energy to my day-by-day existence.

One Saturday I rode over to the filling station where Mat worked, to put air in my bicycle tires. Mat pretended not to notice me as I watched with interest as he cleaned windshields, checked radiators, broke down flats and pumped gas. When I saw him struggling and sweating over a particularly stubborn rim I offered to help. "Can I hold that, Mat?"

"No. Stay out of the way before you get hurt."

He looked through the window toward his boss who was in the office

46

with a customer. Mat didn't want me hanging around because he was afraid Mr. Booth would think he was loafing.

"I'm stronger than you realize. I could help wash cars, too."

"Here," he said irritably. "Get a drink out of the box and take off." He stuffed some change into my hand.

I was glad for the money and the Orange Nehi but hated the way Mat treated me.

The strange thing was the way he seemed to hate me but also protected me. I was hurrying along the outside corridor at the Wynnton School one day when I received a painful jab in the back. I gave a shocked cry, my arm flew up, half my books and papers went scattering across the wet concrete, and the rest were yanked from my arms. I caught my footing and spun around furiously.

Joe Turner was too big and too mean for me to fight. Instead, I stood my distance and demanded, "Give me my papers, Joe!"

"Come getem."

"I'll report you to Mr. Buxton."

He balled his fist. "You asking for a busted lip?"

Helplessly I watched as Joe seized the new notebook and pencils I had just bought, tore and broke them and flung them out onto the soggy ground. My heart racing, I could only hope that I too wouldn't be grabbed by the neck and thrown out into the rain. Finally some doors opened, other students began emerging from the rooms and the bully, driving a sharp punch into my shoulder, spat, "Turd!" and raced on. Hiding my humiliation and tears, I knelt onto the rain-soaked ground and retrieved what remained of my supplies.

The first time Joe Turner bullied me had been in church. We attended the same Sunday School, a small boys' class of about six. I was wearing a new suit, of which I was very proud. It had been a rare Easter gift, only the second suit I'd ever owned. It was light blue and I was certain I looked quite handsome. The Sunday School teacher asked us to bow our heads for prayer, and as he prayed for forgiveness and blessing I felt a light pulsating pressure on my legs. I remained motionless, but opened my eyes slightly and was aghast to see the eraser from the chalkboard, charged with chalk, padding up and down my new trousers, turning them milky white as little puffs of chalk rose to my nose. Horrified, I clamped my eyes shut, held rigid and dared not resist or cause a commotion. Joe Turner meticulously cleaned the eraser on my handsome new pants.

Either the teacher was too intent on his prayer to hear or failed to notice. When heads were raised and eyes opened I took out my handkerchief and, sadness and fear in my throat, tried to brush chalk from my suit. Mr. Preston went right on teaching as though nothing unusual were taking place. A couple of other boys tittered sheepishly. Joe Turner sat with his arms folded, the spent eraser on the floor beneath his chair, an indifferent smirk on his face. He'd gotten by without a single rebuke. I was too afraid to try to stop him, and the teacher had not intervened. The only way I was able to continue Sunday School after that was to make certain I stayed well away from Joe Turner.

Joe was in sixth grade but should have been in seventh. Following his success in attacking me in Sunday School, he'd begun a campaign of bullying. I was getting a drink one day from the water fountain when suddenly my head was slammed down, the nozzle split my lip and water spewed up my nose. As I jerked away sputtering, Joe shoved me aside and calmly dipped his head down to drink.

Nor was the playground a place to avoid humiliation. When I struck out in softball he cried loudly, "The little turd couldn't hit the side of a barn." Never had I felt so demoralized. The one time I responded to Joe, he grabbed me by the shirt, jammed my head against a tree and threatened to bust my nose.

I didn't think of myself as cowardly, but I was truly afraid of Joe Turner—so afraid that going to school each day became a dreadful ordeal. Just to see him out on the school grounds tightened the nerves along my spine. I said nothing to anyone. I didn't want my family thinking me a sissy and I frankly hoped Joe would find another scared kid to bully. But my mother began to suspect something and finally demanded to know why I was dragging my feet every morning.

"You used to like school. Why don't you want to go now?"

"It's okay. I'm not very good at sports."

"Has something happened? I want to know what's going on."

I didn't want to talk about this. Mat and Daddy would be disgusted with me. Eventually I had to tell her about the chalk incident in Sunday School and my troubles with Joe Turner.

"Why is he doing this?" She dragged it out of me. "How long has this been going on?"

Unlike Mama, when Mat heard the story he had no difficulty grasping the situation. "He ever hit you?"

"He knocked me off my bike once."

"Why haven't you told your teacher?" Mama demanded.

"She couldn't do anything. Then he'd really have it in for me!"

Following this embarrassing confession I decided on a desperate plan. I could never confront Joe physically, but it was possible I could outtalk him. He wasn't that bright, was doing very poorly with his second term in sixth grade, and I thought I was smart enough to confuse him. But for several days I couldn't find him at school. Before, I'd been unable to stay out of his way, now I searched the classrooms, the corridors, the grounds before I finally spotted him coming out of the cafeteria. I steeled myself and approached him boldly. "Joe, I don't want to always be fighting you. Why can't we be friends?"

I was prepared for taunting, or even another painful knuckle to the skull. But something stunning occurred. Joe crammed his hands into his pockets. "Sure, Skeeter. I gotta go." He took off, almost running.

After that, Joe more or less dropped out of my life. He didn't come back to church and at school his dodging me became noticeable. I couldn't figure it out, until finally I learned what happened. Mat had come up to the school gunning for Joe. He cornered him, grabbed him by the collar, and threatened to beat the hell out of him if he so much as uttered another word to me. I don't know the words he used, but it was probably something like, "You bother Skeeter again and I'll rip your balls out." Mat had put the fear of the devil in him, and so deeply that I was never harassed by Joe Turner again.

Relieved as I was, I couldn't admit that I needed rescue by my older brother. "You didn't have to do that. I could've talked to him."

"Sure, after you peed in your britches."

I was playing with fire, I knew. My false display of indifference could incite Mat into letting me get battered next time. I clamped my mouth shut but foolishly refused to express gratitude.

* * *

One Saturday morning I collected for the papers, then in the afternoon went to town to pay my bill and see a movie. By the time I left the theater, caught the bus and got off on Wynnton Road and Henry Avenue, darkness had fallen. It had been a Wolfman movie full of blood and gore and my nerves were on edge when I approached the haunted garage. The night was black as the coal in the school basement, and not even a car came along to illuminate the sagging structure. I broke into a run — across the street, down the sidewalk and toward the safety of a street light, a block away. Just as I passed the garage, I heard a loud *thump*! I gave a cry and cleared the next ten feet with a terrified leap. What horror was about to clutch me! This had to be a warning. I ran until the breath was sucked from my chest. Finally I reached our porch, trembling and cold with fear.

I had to talk to someone about my terror of the garage, and naturally that had to be Malcolm Hughley, who'd badgered me into looking through the sagging doors. Malcolm was a big, husky boy. I once stood in his shadow and no part of me could be seen at all. At twelve he already had a masculine voice. I sensed that Malcolm wasn't so much afraid of the garage as intrigued, or maybe even stimulated by my fear. The instant I broached the subject he said cautiously, "That old padlock looks to be about rusted shut. There must be a side or back door. Or maybe whoever uses that dump doesn't need a door."

"I wonder if whatever it is stays in the dark or comes out on moonlit nights, like the Wolfman."

"You can see and hear werewolves," said Malcolm. "I don't know if this thing has a real body."

"But I saw something," I insisted.

"You saw *part* of something. Who knows what form it takes in the inhuman eye?" He looked at me shrewdly. "Maybe you should do something to make a connection."

"What kind of connection?"

"Something to let whatever it is know that you know it's there."

"I think it already knows. The other night I heard a big thump just as I walked by."

"Maybe you should write a note or something."

I knew something had to be done, and Malcolm's idea struck me as an act so courageous, so risky, my hands shook as I undertook it. I sat down and on school tablet paper wrote, "I'm not afraid of you!"

I chose a bright sunlit afternoon on which to approach the garage. Cars sped by. Across the street a small dog, black with white spots, sat on the curb, turning its head to watch people as if patiently waiting for someone to pick him up. An elderly man came down the sidewalk pulling a wagon made of an old crate and some rickety wheels. It didn't seem possible that danger could lurk among such ordinary settings. I parked my bike across the street and walked to the dilapidated double doors.

Beyond the vine-snarled fence that ran around the yard, the two-story white house was sentineled by shaggy trees and tangles of ivy. Never had I observed signs of life in this house, though behind the thick curtains sometimes at night a lamp could be detected, and some of my school chums, who had no interest in the house at all, said, "Of course people live there. I've seen them." I didn't really know if there was a connection between the silent house and the garage, except for a well-trodden dirt path which led from one to the other and which was used, I felt certain, only on ghostly nights.

Satisfied that my message, "I'm not afraid of you!" couldn't be misinterpreted, I ran to the sagging doors and inserted the paper above the padlock with just enough edge revealed that it wouldn't attract the notice of anyone passing by. I ran back to my bike and sped off.

In the next few days I passed coming and going from school and my paper route, and stole a glance at the garage doors for a flicker of my white paper. It remained fixed in the cracks exactly as I had inserted it. Oddly, I felt a kind of letdown. Apparently, my brief surge of courage was useless.

Then late one afternoon as I returned home I noticed that the note had been moved. It was still in the doors but at a different spot. I struggled to determine how it possibly could have dropped down below the heavy padlock. My first impulse was to hurry on, but I had to know whether someone had moved the note, or whether some peculiar trick of gravity had merely allowed it to slip down. Finally I ran to the doors, grabbed the paper and ran back to my bike.

The first thing I saw was that it had been refolded not as I had folded it. With hands trembling I opened the note. It was indeed the one I'd left. At the top, my bold, "I'm not afraid of you!" remained as I had written it. But some writing had been added beneath. The message was brief, and in a delicate hand which could have been meant for no one but me.

It said, "Hello, Skeeter."

* * *

For days I was too mystified and anxious to tell anyone about my espionage. Finally, I showed Malcolm my note and the answer. He looked at me in horror.

"This thing—whatever it is—knows your *name*?"

"Yes. How could this be?"

"I don't know. Maybe spirits know everything."

"What should I do?"

"You'll have to decide. But I warn you to be careful."

With no help from Malcolm, I tried to reassure myself. "It's just an old garage full of junk."

He shot me an oblique glance. "But you saw something, remember?"

"Then what do you think it could be?"

"I can't tell you. All I can say is, it's really weird."

I decided it did no good to talk to Malcolm. Maybe the more my fear was verbalized the greater the danger. I hid the note in the small treasure box in my tent.

* * *

As if risking the shadowy streets in the middle of the night weren't enough, T-Tom, Charlie and I found other ways to court danger. Why was fear ominous and irresistible? Why did we endure disturbed, tossing sleep after seeing a Frankenstein movie, yet couldn't wait until the next one came out? And the Wolfman was worse. A regular guy you might encounter at a service station or as a clerk at Sears, he turned into a vicious monster on full-moon, with ravishing canine teeth, a bristling wolf-like beard, and long ripping claws. My fear of the Frankenstein-like old garage was real, my fears of the unknown in general were real, but why like most everyone else I enjoyed getting scared I couldn't explain. It seemed we were addicted to fascinating horror as long as we knew that between screen and airways was a certain separation through which no malevolent force could reach us.

One of our thrilling voyages was to choose a dark moonless night on which to ride our bikes out to the new municipal airport. Until recently, dignitaries and businessmen had departed on puddle jumpers from Kings Airport out on Victory Drive, a grass field with a long tubular sack mounted on a high pole to inform pilots the direction of the wind. But now we had a new modern municipal airport and Charlie, T-Tom and I rode our bikes out after dark to thrill our nerves on the big incoming planes. We were explorers, the streets were safe, and we had the night vision of cats.

"What time does the big plane come?" T-Tom asked.

"About eight-fifteen." I was usually the one most dependable about schedules and time-frames. "Weather's clear. Should be pretty much on time."

"Reckon somebody'll spot us?" asked Charlie. "I'd hate to run and leave my bike."

"We'll hide them in the trees," I said, "and if we hear anything we'll run the other way."

As we rode, it was just about completely dark, a special kind of blackness as though the world ended at the runway. The black sky made our adventure all the better, we knew the big Delta engines would rip the night with an ear-shattering roar from which we would guard our ears with implanted fingers. The airport was not enclosed by fences and the closest houses were hundreds of yards away.

As cars passed from both directions we hugged the shoulder of the road, and then when no headlights glimmered behind or before us, we pedaled like mad the last couple of hundred yards, whipped off the road, plunged across the ditch and hid our bikes in the bushes. We trudged through the spongy weeds to the bottom of the slope, and paused a moment to catch our breath. The landing strip was elevated, the banks on all sides grassed, and the landing lights ranked the full length of the runway.

We hiked along the tilt of the slope, well beyond the lights of passing cars out on the road, until we came directly in line with the middle of the runway. Stealthy and silent as criminals, we climbed up the bank, knowing our voices could carry a long way across the open spaces, and whispering only when necessary. At the top of the elevation were about twenty or thirty yards of flat shoulder, and then the east end of the runway, the soft undulations of the asphalt bluishly illuminated by the ground lights darting like directional arrows down either side.

The pinpricks of daring and risk spiked the hairs on my arms as the three of us took our positions flat on our backs at the very end of the asphalt. We were not oblivious to the danger of incoming airplanes. A couple of years before, to celebrate the opening of the new terminal, eight Delta officials flew into Columbus for the dedication. As their planes approached the runway a small aircraft somehow met them on a collision course. Feeling the impact, the Delta pilot tried to lift and turn the big airliner. The pilot of the small one-engine plane attempted the same turn. The tangled airplanes crashed, scattering engines and wings and human parts down the runway. It was a sad day for the inaugural flight, a sorrowful day for the families of the nine people who lost their lives, and a bitter blow for Columbus and Delta Airlines. The story made national news, and every time we pulled this stunt, lying spread-eagle on the end of the same runway, we never failed to think about the Delta tragedy.

"I hear 'er," said T-Tom.

"Yea, she's making her turn," contributed Charlie.

We watched the big passenger plane arc into its final approach, and a few miles out, coming straight toward us, the bright landing lights blazed on. Spellbound, eyes startled wide, we lay motionless, not daring to move. We saw the huge wheels come down, the airliner roaring closer and closer and then, not twenty yards above us, the blinking reflective belly seeming so close we could reach up and touch it, the Delta roared over us and a second later the giant tires bit into the macadam with a piercing shriek. Still tense, holding our breath, we felt silence close over us as if the sheer force and defiance of gravity sucked all the air from our little defenseless space.

"Damn if it wasn't close that time," said T-Tom.

"Do you think the pilots ever see us?" Charlie said.

"Naw, they're too busy landing the big bastard."

"Well, we'd better get out of here," I said. "If someone did see and report us we'd be in hot water."

"We'd be up shit creek," said Charlie.

We ran and stumbled back through the grass to our bikes. We pushed out to the road and hid in the ditch until the cars had cleared, and then we scrambled out and sped home.

5

How Mat felt about the possibility of our daddy losing his job I didn't know. Mat seldom expressed his feelings about anything. At sixteen, he felt he could make his own way with help from no one, and with no obligation to provide help for anyone. Any emotion I witnessed from him came mostly from his relations with girls, or from his anger. The combination was volatile.

One afternoon I rode my bike over to Columbus High to get a book out of the car which Mat had driven to school. There was a commotion on the grounds and I hurried over to see what was going on. My blood pressure took a dizzying plunge when I saw it was Mat in a vicious fight with a two-hundred-pound linebacker whose name was Knox Cummings. Instinctively I knew it must have had something to do with Mat's girl Margaret Howell. A large crowd, mostly boys, surrounded them. Just as I plunged into the crowd Mat took a blow to the chin and went down. He lay on his back dazed. I tried to get to him but some boy, a friend I guess, held me back. "Aw, he's all right."

In seconds Mat was on his feet again, but by now some teachers were hurrying across the grounds and the spectators broke up. Half dazed, and supported by a couple of boys, he spat, "I'll see you tonight!" a promise to resume the fight off the school grounds. As he turned away from Knox Cummings he caught sight of me, gave me one cold look and pushed on.

My stomach in turmoil, I ran to the car, got my book and hurried away, tense with worry. No matter how fearless Mat was, he could be no match for this big gorilla. When he came home he barely spoke, which wasn't unusual. He pulled out his trumpet and began practicing as though nothing had happened. Behind his mask of indifference, though, I could see an intensity, which suggested that he was thinking about the fight, perhaps calculating his strategy. All evening the tension built up. Finally after dinner, as he dressed to go out, I slipped up to him. "I don't see why you have to fight Knox again."

He looked at me sharply. "What do you know about it?"

"I heard you tell him."

"Just keep your mouth shut, Skeeter."

"He's too big for you."

"Don't you say a word."

There was a hard rigid line of his jaw and I realized nothing was going to stop him. He'd washed his hair and scrubbed it dry with a towel. Why would a boy about to engage in a bloody fight wash and preen himself? Maybe because this was an event, an occasion to make a statement. Then I realized it was something more. His intent must be to protect his claim on Margaret Howell—a sort of animal instinct for territory. I could imagine him in his fresh shirt and neat haircut, his perfect white teeth and dark brows, dragging home half-broken and covered with blood.

"Is Margaret coming?"

"I told you to keep quiet, Skeeter."

"Where's it going to be?"

"None of your business."

"Mat, don't go. It's crazy."

He clamped his mouth shut. A short time later some boys drove up, blew their horn, and he rushed out.

All evening I could hardly keep my mind on anything else. I read Joanie a story and rocked her to sleep. I finished my homework and looked over my *Columbus Ledger* receipt book. I laid out my clothes for tomorrow—anything to calm my nerves. Finally I turned out the light and went to bed. I had just begun to fall asleep when Mat came in and undressed. I couldn't see how battered he was or hear groans that would evidence my worst fears. I sat up and whispered, "What happened?"

He didn't answer at first. "Nothing. Knox didn't show up."

"You didn't fight?"

"Nothing happened, Skeeter. Just keep quiet about this."

He refused to discuss it, but a few days later I ran into Cooter Fortune, one of Mat's friends, who told me about it. Astounded that this skinny freshman would spoil for a fight against him a second time, Knox Cummings had simply backed off. He sent word that Mat could have Margaret Howell, evidencing some sort of grudging respect which pretty much qualified them as distant yet deferential enemies for the remainder of the school year.

"Who do you think would've won?" I asked.

"Nobody wins in fights like this," said Cooter. "Knox'll never learn to keep his trap shut."

I was afraid that someday Mat's temper would be fatal. But I had an idea that Margaret derived pleasure from two admirers fighting over her. It seemed to me that her and Mat's relationship was mostly a matter of dodging her parents' disapproval and Mat's rebellious indifference. He was hooked on her but I was convinced that sooner or later she was bound to make him miserable.

* * *

Margaret Howell had long red-gold hair, arched brows and a walk that made me think of a tiger. Like most girls she wore dungarees and ballet shoes, but she declined the short hair styles. She had mysterious caged lashes, eyes as blue as marble and pouting red lips. When they drove around together she slipped over close to Mat and drew his arm over her shoulder, her legs richly crossed or tucked to one side. Her smile was enticingly wicked and desperately sweet.

One night I sat on the edge of the tub watching Mat shave.

"Why don't you bring Margaret here sometimes?"

He scoffed. "To her family our house would look like a dump."

I knew what he meant. Our little two-bedroom was cramped and pathetic, but I admired my father's determination to own his own home and work to get it paid for.

"I'd bring her here anyway," I said. "If she doesn't like it too bad for her."

Mat was a trumpet player in the Columbus High band. In his blue and orange uniform, his shined black shoes, his plumes and hat and braids, he cut a handsome figure. Margaret was a majorette, and the thing I noticed most about her was the way she strutted, with her back erect, planting the balls of her feet first, prancing, as if nothing could be lovelier than her legs, arms, neck and smile.

Mat refused to drive Margaret's car but picked her up in our old 1941 Chevrolet. This must have been the source of some irritation to her parents who counted themselves in the highest social hierarchy of town. Margaret was too infatuated with Mat to allow this to interfere, but I foresaw a heartbreaking mix. My brother, I think, realized the risk he was taking to court a girl whose social awareness was so acute, but he plunged forward like a man addicted.

* * *

By fifth grade I myself had already suffered the pain of rejection. Her name was Judy Rollins, and socially she was about on the scale of Margaret Howell. A black-haired beauty who came to school every day wearing "adorable" dresses and big bows in her hair like a beautifully made-up doll, she was let out of a shining new Buick at the school's front entrance, her cheeks rosy and her laugh musical. She attended dance schools and charm schools. Despite her social heritage, her smile, her gestures and mannerisms were uncondescending, and she didn't come off as too spoiled by her sophisticated upbringing. She had never seen our little house on

Schaul, but she knew Wynnton was a decent, respectable neighborhood and probably would be appalled if she knew we were so poor we could be thrown out of it.

In fourth grade I had begun to practice my skills at drawing horses — horses prancing, horses rearing, horses soaring over jumps. One day Judy whispered to me, "I'd love one of your horses, Skeeter." Delirious with pleasure I labored all week and on Friday presented her with drawings not of one but of seven horses. On the last of these I wrote, "I love you"— a shy and rather reserved declaration of my devotion.

All weekend I thought about Judy. On Monday I kept glancing at her across the classroom hoping she would slip me a note. But she never looked my way. Finally at recess, breathless with torment, I asked her if she liked my horses. "Yes, I did, Skeeter, thank you very much."

This was all. There was no acknowledgment of my lovelorn confession. I stood amazed at the grownup gentility with which she handled a sad moment. Not even a twinkle of the eye, a bit of color in the cheeks suggested the slightest emotional attraction. No other girl measured up to her in beauty, and I knew that it would be a long time before I could let her slip from her pedestal.

Bearing the scars of this wound I realized that I myself had been an instrument of rejection, and in a way this was worse. At Christmas a girl named Trudi Frazier hadn't drawn my name but had elected to give me a present anyway — an elaborate chemistry set, handsomely boxed, with dozens of experiments, a microscope, chemicals and mixing paddles and test tubes and heating torches. "I just wanted to give you a present, Skeeter. I looked for one a long time."

Amazed and embarrassed, I mumbled, "I'm sorry I didn't get you anything, Trudi." Neither I nor my parents could ever have afforded something so elaborate for a schoolmate and of course it had never occurred to me that Trudi Frazier might give me a present.

"Oh, you needn't," she said sweetly. "I hope you enjoy it."

Until that moment I'd had no idea how much Trudi liked me. Unfortunately, science and geography were not my passion, and I hoped she would never suspect that the expensive chemistry set would suffer slow decay on the floor of my crowded closet.

Trudi Frazier was a large girl, big-boned, not delicate like Judy Rollins, with dark, frank eyes, and a faintly freckled nose. She wore plain smart dresses and cashmere sweaters sent over by relatives in Europe. She loved to seesaw and swept up and down laughing, her skirt flowing. She always looked at me with steady, thoughtful eyes. But though I was always nice to Trudi, and thanked her again and again for the chemistry set, I knew little about subterfuge or flattery, and could only express casual friendship. It seemed to me that once she understood she was not going to snag my heart her look became wiser and more somber.

So by fifth grade I had rejected and had been rejected. I harbored a desire to be loved by Judy Rollins, to be liked by Trudi Frazier, and these complex emotions seemed all mixed in with my fears and with the secret yearnings of my heart. I wondered if other kids felt these urges too. I thought they probably did, for Miss Barton commented to us one day, as if she perceived everything but didn't find everything appropriate for the chalkboard, *Hope deferred makes the heart sick.*

* * *

One day Miss Barton was absent, and our substitute Mrs. Weaver, an older woman with gray hair, short stubby fingers and thick round glasses, didn't much care what we did. She gave us busy work, and buried her face in some papers on her desk. It was an easy day for us, the kind we savored, but the class was restless. Pencil in hand, paper before me, I sat gazing out the window, wanting to be outside, and wondering what was going on with my daddy down at Chattahoochee Paint, and what would happen to my little sister without adequate medicine. *An idle mind is the devil's workshop.* It would have been better had Miss Barton been there driving us like slaves.

At break Pigg Hodge said, "Let's go out and shimmy up the flagpole."

"Mr. Buxton would kill us," we all responded.

Mr. Buxton was our principal, whom we all feared. So we said, "Okay, let's go."

We were required to have our recess out back, where there were acres of play area, large shade trees and a summer house from which some of the teachers kept a casual eye and the more studious pupils sat and read. Miss Barton drank coffee and smoked. Cigarettes and coffee, she said, were her vice, but she admonished us so vigorously against them we had little inclination to emulate her.

According to an old catalog, the school's original buildings were located "in the midst of a magnificent grove, high above the level of the city, thus affording the purest air and best of water." In 1890 a structure was erected for males who wore uniforms and were trained in the military fashion. The boys and girls were separated by the large grove of trees to "prevent any intercourse between the two departments...there is not a single saloon within a mile and a half of the grounds." I had no doubt that at Wynnton, especially with Miss Barton, Mr. Buxton and others, we were receiving as good an elementary education as could be found in the country.

Half a dozen of us slipped out through the double yard gate onto the front lawn. The hunch was to see who could shinny up highest on the flagpole. Pigg Hodge was most agile, proficient in wrapping his legs around the pole and inching up little by little. Just about every day Pigg brought an onion sandwich for lunch and, standing downwind, no one ever questioned the contents of his mother's cupboards.

Despite our various levels of academic proficiency, our intimidation by teachers, our fears and hatreds of geography, history or mathematics, I believed that every pupil loved Wynnton School and sustained a certain pride in being a part of it. Wynnton's main entrance was a two-story, pale-green stucco, with great multi-paned windows and wood floors, and single-level C-shaped wings. Exterior corridors were exposed to the north wind, and the cafeteria, the original little red brick building founded in 1843, was reached by crossing an open court. There was a long sweeping driveway and wide steps leading up to the front doors.

Wynnton had played a part in the Civil War. Columbus, Georgia, was known as the site of the last battle, and when the Union army started advancing, the Confederates hid their munitions in some of the school-rooms and camouflaged the road leading up to the school. The blue coats marched right by and never suspected anything. John Stith Pemberton, a pharmacist, received a nasty saber wound in this battle which eventually led him to inventing Coca-Cola as it came to be named.

In the early days it was Wynnton Academy, then Wynnton High and Wynnton College before becoming simply Wynnton School. Everything from kindergarten to four years of college and post-graduate courses in Astronomy, Latin, Anglo Saxon, Elocution and Vocal Music had been taught. By the time my generation came along it had become only an elementary school.

Keeping an eye on the front doors through which Mr. Buxton could come, one by one we jumped as high as we could up onto the flagpole, using our hands and legs, or kicking off shoes to shinny up until we lost courage or strength or grip, at which moment we slid down like firemen. Every boy trusted that if Mr. Buxton came flinging himself through the main entrance we'd explode in such a blur of retreat he'd be able to record no names. Only Pigg ascended fearlessly, convinced that he was already on every teacher's blacklist because he could never learn to spell.

Mr. Buxton was a tall man of angular frame, sparse hair, long stilt-like legs and sharp, chiseled features. The thing he seemed to like most was ringing the school bell. At exactly the appointed hour, to the second, he seized the bell and went up and down the hall signaling whatever the occasion demanded: school in, lunchtime, fire drill, school out. With his scarecrow posture, his hurried, disjointed gait, his bell and his gangly frame Mr. Buxton reminded us of Abraham Lincoln, or of a *Saturday Evening Post* portrait by Norman Rockwell.

Years ago when my brother was in Wynnton, Mr. Buxton had visited my mother to demonstrate how inattentive Mat was. He sat on our sofa turning his head slowly left, slowly right, like a puppet drawn by a lazy string. This, he said, personified Mat's classroom nonchalance. I think it was a relief to my parents when Mat finally passed Wynnton and went on to Columbus High.

Though I was more frightened of Mr. Buxton than of Miss Barton, we all respected him as a man of intellectual honesty. I often wondered if he could explain to me why cruel boys had wired my brother to a tree, or why a man like Mr. Montgomery, who was already rich, would steal more while my father struggled to make ends meet, and why life seemed so fearful to me. But I had neither the boldness nor the words to ask him.

He did not come blasting out to run us off the flagpole and we were almost sorry to retreat back into the classroom without high drama.

6

One or two afternoons a week Miss Barton read to us from *Remi*, sometimes assuming an English accent. We knew she would like nothing better than to slip on her sturdy walking shoes and explore remote Alpine villages and valleys. Two or three days a week we practiced our script, incorporating one of her proverbs, *A stitch in time saves nine*.

When Mr. Buxton rang the final bell there was a collective sigh of relief. Those who had ridden bicycles to school hastened to the racks. Jack stood at the iron gates, urging students to clear the exits. Boys took off their belts to strap books together; girls tied sweaters about their waists. Those who had received bad cards (the worst fate that happened to a Wynnton student; bad cards must be signed and returned by parents, and there was no greater source of humiliation) skulked across the grounds looking at their shoelaces.

Sometimes instead of walking home by the old garage on Henry Avenue, I'd join a part-time friend Russell Ladder who was in Mrs. Henderson's fifth grade class and lived on Ada Avenue. I think what drew me to Russell was that his father had left one job and accepted another, and it seemed he had the privilege of picking and choosing.

"It's that simple for your father to get a job?" I said.

"Yeah. Engineers are in demand."

Russell and I both had little sisters, mine two, his barely a year. His mother and father both worked, and upon arriving home, Russell was greeted only by the young girl caring for his baby sister. I always counted on my mother being home and thought how empty his house must feel to him.

"She doesn't like me," Russell said.

"Who?"

"Cindy. The girl who keeps Elli, my baby sister. I hate going home when she's there."

Russell Ladder was several inches taller than I, and seemed to grow in spurts. In December he held fast, in January shot up, then in spring held fast again. His clothes never quite fit, nor were they as neat as they might be. He was something of a visionary, though he struggled to find words to express himself and the less he succeeded the more frustrated he became. "I can't even tell my mother about Cindy," he said. "Cindy likes the baby but she's mean to me."

I had met the sitter once, a plain young woman with straight, honey-colored short hair and a glance that appeared wistful and distant. She came in the morning and remained until Mrs. Ladder returned from work in the afternoon, hovering over the baby. Even when Russell picked Elli up, Cindy walked back and forth nervously, as though she resented the intrusion. It was as if in a way the child had become hers, and he was an outcast. "When she thinks nobody's listening she croons to the baby," said Russell, "but around me she clams up. Someday I'll get the axe and kill her."

"Then you'd spend the rest of your life in jail."

"What difference does it make?"

"If it's that bad I don't see why you can't tell your mother."

I liked Mrs. Ladder. She was tall like Russell, with healthy red lips and a large mouth. She wore rings on several fingers and drove her own car. She worked with a group of lawyers and spent a good deal of time in the courthouse. When she arrived home each afternoon she dismissed Cindy immediately, planted hugs and kisses on the baby and asked Russell

67

about his day and his homework. Their weekends were mostly devoted to long family drives to relatives in the country.

One afternoon as I returned home from delivering papers, I decided to ride by and see Russell. To my astonishment there was a police cruiser in front of their house. I pedaled hard and arrived just as Russell rushed out the front door. He saw me and ran over. "She took the baby! I knew I should kill her!"

"What are you talking about?"

"My little sister. Cindy's run off with her!"

I could hardly grasp it. The only kidnapping I'd ever heard of was the Lindbergh case and that was before I was born.

"How do you know? Maybe they're just lost somewhere."

"Some of the baby's clothes are gone. Her bottles. One of our suit-cases."

Through the open front door I could hear Mrs. Ladder crying. There was so much tension and hysteria in the air I felt my hands gripping the handlebars tighter and tighter.

"She stole Elli and ran away!" Russell spat. "The police have been to Cindy's house. She's cleared out!" He balled his fists. "Probably she wants money."

"Money?"

"They take children for money."

He was struggling not to cry. I could imagine the baby wondering where her mother was and, afraid I might cry too, I said hastily, "She'll be back, Russell. I know you'll get Elli back."

With a sudden desire to see my own sister, I jumped onto my bike and flew home. The instant I ran in I exclaimed, "Russell's little sister's been kidnapped!"

My mother stared at me. "Calm down and tell me what you're talking about."

I told them about little Elli.

"She'll hide her somewhere and demand ransom," said Mat.

I shuddered to think what the sitter might do if she became desperate and had to get Elli off her hands.

I ran in to see Joanie playing with toys. "Hey, Joanie ..." If anyone took Joanie I would kill them, too. I, who wept for a poor man like Jack, for a fallen bird or a little child trapped in a well—I could have such thoughts.

Overnight, the kidnapping became news. Reporters and police pieced together part of the story. The babysitter Cindy Atwood was twenty years old. She had no relatives in Columbus, having arrived from South Carolina after a bitter dispute with her family. She had dropped out of school and run off with a boy who promised her the world. At seventeen she became pregnant and carried the baby three months, until she miscarried. When the boy abandoned her, Cindy found herself alone with nowhere to go and no one to rely on. How she ended up in Columbus was unclear. She had no money but was somehow able to arrange for a room in a boarding house run by a matronly woman who took pity on her. It was her benefactress who introduced her to Mrs. Ladder and who, following the kidnapping, assured the police she was a harmless girl, lonely and lost, but not bad.

Russell didn't come to school and we all anguished over what was happening. One horrible boy mused, "She'll probably kill her."

"But why!"

"Because then when they catch her they won't be able to prove anything."

At school we were all animated and excited. Miss Barton warned us, "Don't let your emotions make you physically ill. Pay attention to your work."

We wondered how the sitter got away with the child. "She had to travel by bus," one boy reasoned. "That means the baby, clothes, the buggy—a lot of stuff."

"Maybe she cut her up and buried her in a box," one boy said.

Coming home from my paper route I rode by the evil old garage and turned my eyes toward it fully for the first time since I'd retrieved my note. My stare was uncharacteristically heroic. "Just don't try this on me!" I said.

The drama came to a startling climax in two days. Cindy was found, the baby was safe. A photograph in *The Ledger* showed her making her tearful confession. She had taken Elli to her boardinghouse, where she collected her belongings. She walked aimlessly for hours, and ended up finally at the home of a friend, to whom she fed the concocted story that she'd been told to keep the baby overnight. As soon as the friend heard the truth on the news she demanded that Cindy return at once to the Ladders or contact the police. Cindy pleaded for one day to call the baby her own. She had no one to love, no one to love her, she just wanted little Elli for a while all on her own. We assumed she must be a little crazy. When the next day she made her way back to the Ladders she walked through a gathering of distressed friends and family and dropped the baby into Mrs. Ladder's arms. She then threw herself into a chair and sobbed uncontrollably. Mrs. Ladder finally put her arms around her.

"What'll happen to her now?" I asked Russell.

He shrugged. "I guess I won't axe her."

"Probably they'll send her to jail."

"Maybe not. My parents are refusing to press charges."

"They're not going to do anything?"

"Try to get her some help. She needs it."

Despite their ordeal, the Ladders forgave Cindy. I was amazed. Still, their lives were changed. Russell's mother quit her job, and remained home with her children. I was amazed even more that they could give up a big part of their income, and still do well. I wished Daddy were something more than a clerk in a store, but I knew he had always made the best of his circumstances. At least I saw that riches protected no one from bad things.

Having survived his short-lived celebrity, Russell himself seemed more relaxed and outgoing, though still too remote for our friendship to last.

* * *

The friend I did have a long-running relationship with was John Shoulder, who lived with his family on the lower end of Henry Avenue. Their house had brick foundations with two access openings closed only by misfitting plywood doors. In summer, to avoid the suffocating heat outside, John and I occasionally crawled under the house where there was plenty of room and the dirt was black and cool. It was like walking out of the sun into a cave smelling of earth and moisture. We could draw a ring and play marbles, but mostly we just talked. I lamented my increasingly desperate need for a bicycle. "If I can't figure a way to get one, I'll be grounded. Then how am I going to earn money?"

"You'll get one," said John, the optimist. "Things work out." Overhead pipes ran along the bottom of the joists and light penetrating from above revealed holes insects and rodents could easily squeeze through. The yards were mowed, the garage held no food products, but the uninsulated floors and walls presented a likely environment for rats—which was a terror to Mrs. Shoulder. A family of mice had taken up residence in the house, and her horror of them had assumed hysterical proportions.

Mrs. Shoulder was a usually calm, friendly woman with straw-blond hair and inquisitive and tolerant hazel eyes. To her, everyone, no matter how young or old, had the right of expression, of thought, and no child was too immature to offer enlightenment to her adult world. This was her approach with John, her only son, and with me and his other friends. He had a mind; he was capable of knowing right and wrong and it was unnecessary for her to monitor his every move. She afforded John both independence and space, and assumed him intelligent enough to take responsibility for his actions. Consequently John, a year older than I, was mature beyond his age in a thoughtful, self-sufficient way.

I found Mrs. Shoulder easy to talk to. She listened to my observations and responses with no indication that a fifth grader could impart nothing of value to her. Her voice remained calm, never condescending and never panicky except when it came to mice.

"I will not," she stated matter-of-factly, "I will not share my home or my kitchen with those disgusting creatures."

"They slip in from outside," said Mr. Shoulder, who was both fond of and amused by his wife. "I will protect you, my love. Besides, they demand very little of us."

"You will get rid of the mice or you will get rid of me."

One day I was in their front yard waiting for John to come home when Mrs. Shoulder walked out and sat on the porch smoking. Between us four or five robins lit in the grass, and on a whim I decided to see just how close I could come to them. As I crept toward the birds Mrs. Shoulder observed me silently. To catch a bird on the ground is no little feat, and this was a challenge of stealth and concentration. After several cautious steps I leaned forward, extended my arm and slowly closed my fingers on a robin's tail. The reaction was as explosive and violent as a small bird is capable of. It screeched and fluttered so wildly I jumped back defensively. "You had him!" said Mrs. Shoulder. Her tone was approving, so I felt compelled to help her with the mice.

After failure with bait and poison inside and out, it was determined that the mice lived in the motor compartment of their refrigerator. Twice one had been seen scurrying behind the box, but when Mr. Shoulder dragged the fridge away from the wall no mouse emerged. "Darn thing's full of insulation. Perfect place for a nest," he said.

"A nest! A nest! That means more mice!"

Mr. Shoulder appropriated a shovel, a yard rake, a hoe and a couple of sturdy brooms. Then he instructed each of us, Mrs. Shoulder, John and me, to take a position with one of these weapons while he himself commandeered the shovel which he stood close against the wall. Their kitchen was large, with doors leading into the dining room and halls, linoleum floors and cabinets all the way down one side, the refrigerator, a small dinette table and chairs, upright oven, a sink under the window. All the chairs were removed from the table so Mr. Shoulder could position us in a rough circle around the kitchen.

"What are we going to do?" John asked.

"Try to run them out and have a whack at them."

Mrs. Shoulder grasped a broom in both her hands. "Just let one come my way!"

I had a shovel, John the rake. Mr. Shoulder took hold of the refrigerator and worked it out from the wall. "Watch now. You'll have only one chance."

He removed the motor cover and, with a thin switch from a bush outside, began jabbing and probing into the motor and pipes, at the same time hammering on the side with his free hand, kicking and thumping.

I could never have imagined that mice could be so fast. Two flashed across the floor in a blur. I swung at one and struck the linoleum at least two feet behind it. Another shot by John, practically between his legs, and his thrust missed totally. Mr. Shoulder grabbed his shovel but got no shot at all. With cries of disgust we turned to see that Mrs. Shoulder was standing smack in the middle of the kitchen table. How she achieved this feat could be explained only by some supernatural force. Panic must have pumped such action into her legs that from a solid, spread-foot stance on the floor she sprang, catlike, without taking a step—a levitation she couldn't possibly have accomplished under ordinary conditions. There she was, standing upright in the middle of the dinette table, broom held at the same ready poise, face utterly drained of color.

With every effort to keep a straight face, Mr. Shoulder walked quietly over to the table, carefully removed the broom from her hands and gently asked, "Wouldn't it be difficult, my dear, to hit anything from up there?"

She stared down at him with a cold and frozen glint. Amazed, we held motionless, then we could restrain ourselves no longer. We fell backward, hysterical with laughter. It was only after much persuasion that she finally extended her hand and allowed herself to be helped down.

The mice were eventually extinguished with traps, a simple device upon which the genius of modern engineering has not improved. From the animal shelter the Shoulders rescued a mixed breed cat, a flecked-haired black and gray whose name was Sooty, who quickly developed into an efficient mouser and thereafter kept the old house under quarantine.

All the way home I giggled, remembering Mrs. Shoulder standing stark in the middle of the table as from some superhuman feat of acrobatics, and imagining Miss Barton in her firm strong hand writing on the chalkboard, *A miss is as good as a mile.*

* * *

It was right after the incident with the mice that near disaster struck. John was a free thinker, somewhat aloof from the rest of us. While we were climbing trees he was inventing new ways to make a slingshot pistol. While we were gathering up enough chums for softball he was trying to run a wire conduit between two points to make a telephone. He had inquisitive, amused eyes, a slow tentative walk and he tilted his head slightly, eyes narrowed, as though contemplating some idea or possibility. He had plans to make Eagle Scout and to earn every merit badge there was. Already he'd begun to work on his woodcarving badge and almost every day practiced with his scout knife. He had carved a pretty rubber band gun, with which he was a dead shot.

John and I were sitting in a chinaberry tree on the edge of a thicket not far from our houses. He pulled out a pouch and two sleek-looking pipes. "Where'd you get those?" I asked.

"Carved them. Corn cobs."

"They don't look like corn cobs to me."

"I hollowed them out. Shaved them. Sanded. Stained. Plugged the bottoms. Pretty neat, huh?"

"Corn cob pipes?"

"Yeah. Like Huck Finn. And this here," he said with a drawl, "is rabbit tobacco."

He proceeded to stuff both pipes, lit one and passed it to me then lit the other. "Just suck into your mouth. You don't have to inhale. I added a little ginger to make it sweet."

I sucked tentatively through the stem he'd made of reed, and broke out in a hacking cough.

He laughed, then narrowed his eyes. "You ever gonna really smoke?"

"No," I said.

"Why not?"

"It's a sin."

"Ride by church some Sunday and see if you can stir the smoke around those big white columns."

"I don't have to ride by," I said, remembering that my daddy was one of those smokers between Sunday School and church. "I'm there. You should be, too."

"I tried a Tiparillo once," said John. "A friend of my mother's left it in our ashtray. What do you think of a lady with long painted red nails smoking a cigar?"

I reflected a moment. "I wouldn't want to kiss her," I said.

"Ah! Good answer, Skeeter. Surprised you didn't say she's a sinner."

About a week after our corncob smoking, John nearly killed himself with his knife. I had walked through the front door of his house—no one ever locked their doors—and found him sitting on his kitchen floor trimming a piece of wood. His cousin Bland sat in a chair watching. Bland was a studious kid, as smart as John, skinny, wearing glasses, his shirt tail hanging out. John had the stick between his legs drawing the knife down, and just as I entered the kitchen Bland cried, "Oh, my God!"

I was similarly shocked as I saw the wood slip, the knife plunge down and the blade slice right through John's pants into his leg. Blood gushed, and in an instant his pants were soaked. A swooping nausea twisted in my stomach. He sat staring at the red flow as though fascinated or shocked, until finally his cheeks and hands turned white, and he began gnawing his lips.

"Do something!" Bland cried.

Blood was going everywhere, staining the floor, running under the table. John stood, rushed to the bathroom and jumped into the tub. In a flash I realized it was like John to throw himself into the tub rather than ruin his mother's floor. "Skeeter," he said, "hand me a towel."

Dumbly, I grabbed a towel from the rack and threw it to him. He tied a tourniquet around his thigh as Bland ran to the phone and started trying furiously to contact I knew not who.

Just as it swept through my mind that he could bleed to death, in walked Mrs. Shoulder. As far as I knew, only Divine Providence could have brought her home at this moment. She hardly ever returned before the end of the day. In one sweep she took in the blood on the floor, the trail leading to the bathroom and John standing in the tub, bleeding through his pants. She cried, "My God, John! What happened?"

"Cut," he said. "Knife."

Not so much as stripping off his pants to look, she grasped him by the arm, hauled him out to the car and sped off to the emergency room. Dropping the receiver into the cradle, Bland looked as if he were going to be sick. Then he recovered and muttered, "I guess we oughta try and clean up." He began foraging through their pantry to find some cleaning material. On our knees, we wiped down the linoleum and the bloody trail down the hallway, then rinsed out the tub.

"You don't think he'll die do you?" I asked.

Bland clamped his lips tightly.

Scared as I was about John I admired his steel nerves and wished I had such courage. As soon as we finished cleaning I ran home to tell Mama, then an hour or so later I had to hurry off to throw papers. I found myself taking great care, as though something awful could happen to me too. When I had finished my long route and got back home, John telephoned me. "They took twenty-one stitches," he said matter of factly. "It was a vertical cut down the side."

"We cleaned up your blood," I said.

"Yeah, I saw. The doctor said if you're going to cut yourself, the thigh muscle is the best place." He laughed. "Thank goodness the knife didn't go between my legs."

"Does it hurt?"

"Just beginning to. He told me not to ride until the stitches come out. Devil," said John, "I bet I can pedal with one leg."

"We'll build you a wheelchair," I said, "out of your old scooter wheels. I can roll you around."

"I'm planning to walk stiff-legged, you know? So people will notice. Might as well get *something* outa this."

I kept thinking about all that blood, that he could have died right before my eyes, and wondering if the evil garage just blocks away had reached out to get me and got him instead.

* * *

I was wheeling down a steep hill on my paper route when my chain slipped the sprocket and I had no brakes. Gathering speed by the second, I could see nothing below but trees and cars rushing along the intersecting street. To my left was a low bank and grassy yard. I decided to throw myself down before it was too late, and pray to the angels of mercy. When I hit the ground hard my bike went one way, my bag of papers another, and I still another. I tumbled and spun across the grass, trying to keep my limbs loose, and seeing my papers, as though through a movie reel in slow motion, flying and sweeping like birds down the sidewalk and out into the street. It was a sunny but frigid day, my fingers and toes were already tingling from cold, and bruised and mortified I pulled myself to my knees and sat miserable, swearing with curse words whose true meaning I hardly knew.

I stood at last, gave my bike a swift kick and set it on its stand. This was the third time the old Schwinn had slipped the chain, though never before under such dangerous conditions. I was struggling to right the chain and sprocket when an elderly man walked out from a nearby house. He summed up my predicament and evidently saw the misery in my face. "Any way I can help, son?"

"If I had a screwdriver…"

"I'll see what I can do." He went back into the house, limping a little, and returned with a screwdriver.

I reset the chain and made sure I had brakes, and then returned the screwdriver and thanked him. As I began to gather my papers and stuff them into the canvas bag he moved along, bending with effort to help me. "Would you like a paper?" I asked. "I have extras."

"You sure?"

"I usually just trash a few anyway."

"Then, yes, thank you."

This was the second time in recent weeks that I had witnessed an act of kindness. I was always wishing and waiting for something big to happen, now it occurred to me that a lot of little things made something big, and I should be thankful.

I finally finished throwing the papers and got back to the corner of Wynnton Road and Henry Avenue about the time Daddy exited the bus, which he rode when Mat needed the car. I'd noticed two brand-new bikes in the window of Wynnton Pharmacy, a blue and white boy's and a sleek red girl's, and as I joined Daddy to walk home, pushing my bike, I said, "Did you see those new Schwinns in the window?"

"I didn't notice them, Skeeter."

"Twenty-six inch. Blue and red with white trim. Perfect for my route."

I was hoping for some encouragement, perhaps even for a promise, but when I glanced at Daddy's face I was sorry I'd said anything. I knew the possibility of getting a new bike without help from my parents was pretty slim, but I knew too that he would need every cent if he lost his job. I was both miffed that my parents couldn't help me and ashamed that I put more pressure on him.

Daddy himself used to ride a pony from their Alabama farm to school. The idea fascinated me and I asked him about it.

"Did you ride your pony in every kind of weather?"

"Rain, sun, storms. About five miles each way."

"You just tied him up and made him wait?"

"He was used to it. That was a long time ago, Skeeter. We didn't have school buses back then." I could see he wasn't eager to recall those harsh days. Winter storms and blistering sun were as hard on him and his pony as they were on me and my broken-down bike.

I had recently become aware of something else, too. Mat's bike was missing. I knew where he kept it beside the garage, I knew he hadn't accidentally left it somewhere and that nobody ever borrowed it. Finally I asked him where his bike was.

"Oh, I ditched it," Mat said.

"You *ditched* it! That was a good bike!"

"Yeah, at one time."

"I bet you sold it—for practically nothing."

He shrugged but didn't answer.

So now even this possible backup was gone, and all I could think of was the wonderful new bicycles in the pharmacy window, and of the bitterly cold days ahead.

7

Every night we waited anxiously for Daddy to come home and tell us whether he had a job. The fear of losing his salary ran deep and wove a frightening thread through our daily lives. We were having dinner when he described some men who'd come into the store.

"What did they want?" Mama asked.

"I don't know. They all left with shotguns."

"A payoff," said Mat.

Now that Mat and I knew about Daddy's troubles at Chattahoochee Paint it was discussed openly, though not without the renewed caution that nothing went out of the room.

"Why don't they ever get caught?" I asked.

"Because there's a whole bunch who're covering it up," Daddy said.

"Why can't you just write a secret letter?"

"That's a coward's way. If Monty's caught, that could be the end of the store and me too."

Daddy worked hard, doing everything he could to make extra money, moonlighting most nights and weekends. He and my Uncle Talbot added on rooms, enclosed garages, and contracted for all kinds of renovation work. Daddy had always said that someday he would have a store of his own. He wanted to be free to use his own imagination, his own management, answering to himself and has family. I guess it was every man's dream, to be self-employed. But it took money and courage, and perhaps a little push.

Mama said, almost accusingly, "I have to pay Dr. Ward next week. I can't ask him to keep sending medicine." I didn't know how she thought Daddy could do more but there was no mistaking the tone in her voice.

Joanie was too little to understand any of this but I looked over at her and saw a little frown on her forehead. She must have picked up on the tension in the room.

Daddy sighed. "Maybe we can finish the job this weekend and get paid."

As soon as dinner was over I ran to my small treasury hidden in the bottom of our cluttered closet and brought out the cigar box which I had meticulously wrapped in tin foil. I laid out the bills by denomination, knowing by heart how many bills there were—how many tens, five and ones. With dismay I realized that my little savings wouldn't do much. The worst of Joanie's kidney infection was over, but antibiotics were expensive and Dr. Ward, a small neighborhood pharmacist, patient and considerate as he was, could ill afford to carry accounts very long.

I put the cigar box back in the closet, slipped on my jacket, and went out to sit on our front steps. The spear-shaped bayonet trees on the vacant lot next to ours looked like knights in armor, guarding a castle in motion-less silence. Night shadows formed by street and porch lights slithered down columns and trees into puddles of blackness.

I worried as much about Mama as I did about Daddy. Several times a week she struggled to roll our old-fashioned washing machine from the back porch into the kitchen where she could hook it up to water and the sink drain. She hung out clothes on a line strung between posts in the backyard. When she wasn't washing or cooking she sat at the sewing machine pumping the floor pedal making Joanie's clothes or shirts for Mat and me. Occasionally she was able to splurge and manage the ingredients to make wonderful chocolate fudge. She hardly spent any of the little money Daddy managed to give her on herself—she gave everything to the care of her children. I thought she tried to make the best of life but was haunted by lost dreams, by what might have been.

Mama's love for her six siblings, and theirs for us, was a strong strain that ran through our families. As next to the youngest, she'd had to go to work at the age of thirteen, as her older brothers and sisters had. She was seventeen when she married. There were few photograph albums around our house, but in a drawer somewhere was a picture of Mama and Daddy at about that age and I thought them a truly handsome couple. There seemed to me, though, a faint look of sadness in her eyes.

Her mother, my grandmother, lived only a couple of blocks away and nearly every day Mama bundled up Joanie and walked over to see her. My grandmother spent most of her days sitting in a rocking chair knitting beautiful, intricate doilies.

When Mama had a chance to sit down she picked up a book, a paperback or a romance, a historical novel or some biography. With a book half open in her lap, her eyes unfocused, she would get a dreamy, faraway look on her face. I suspected she had visions of a life grander than the one she'd been dealt, and given the opportunity she might have expanded her thoughts and mind. "Life can be disappointing," she said, "but that doesn't mean we should underestimate ourselves." It seemed to me that her prodigious reading served her well in lieu of a formal education. I admired her courage and forgiving spirit but hoped I wouldn't grow up with unfulfilled dreams as she had.

One by one neighborhood doors closed, lights blinked off. Dogs scratched at trash cans, the whippoorwill called, the broken sounds of a far-off radio clattered along the rooftops, a plane passed overhead, a car door slammed, a teenager hurrying home late shouted out—these were all sounds I knew well. I listened to the coupling of railcars three miles away and a sadness stole over me, a sadness so profound I understood it couldn't have come from life, but from the universe I breathed, a sadness that was not emotion but emptiness and fear.

So far in my mind, life was a vague, dreamy affair, without beginning or end. My family's struggles for money, my brother's rebellion, my fear of the old garage, all made me take everything seriously, and yearn every day for something that would warm me with life's cheerful, lively heat. I sustained a fantastic belief that something special would happen, a sharpening of the reflexes, a sense of heightened awareness which would define me as an individual and provide direction for my future.

And I counted on things getting better. How they would get better I didn't know, any more than I knew why they were bad in the first place. I understood that there were elements over which one had no control, some good, some bad, some threatening, some nourishing, but all of which had to be negotiated with caution like walking barefoot through a path of shattered glass. These elements I wanted to grasp and embrace, add some or take some away, in a manner which would harm me and those I loved least, with the ultimate result of making things better. I wanted control over my destiny, but there was a kind of freedom, too, in realizing that all I could really do was hope my responses to fate's impersonal directions would be useful and fulfilling.

I listened to the short warning toot of a switch engine and wondered what it was in me that kept pressing forward, catching glimpses of grand possibilities. I feared that there would always be within me something un-satisfied, and wondered if after all I had inherited my mother's melancholy.

Even so, there was a special pleasure in sitting quietly to listen to the town operating all around me while I myself remained removed from it. I looked up at the sky where stars flickered like specks of glitter on black poster paper, and waited for the sadness and fear to go away.

* * *

I had just arrived home from collecting for my papers when Mama met me at the door. "I'm sorry, Skeeter, your tent burned down."

I stared at her.

"Some of your friends came over. They lit a candle …"

I ran to the backyard. All that was left of my sturdy green tent were ashes, a few shreds of rope, a couple of pegs—this and an ugly hole full of mud and water. The boys had tried to extinguish the flames with a garden hose, but it was obvious that my prized possession had gone up quickly. The garage wall was scorched but not burned.

I jumped down and searched feverishly. Nothing was left, not even my treasure box where I'd secreted some of my prized possessions—a ring Jean Gresham had given me, a silver dollar, a few comic book cutouts, a scout knife, and the secret note, "I'm not afraid of you," with its spooky response, "Hello, Skeeter." Finally I found the silver dollar, charred but usable, but it did little to stop my tears.

I sank down into the cold grass. I'd brought this on myself. Obviously, the boys had not meant to burn down my tent. We often lit candles. I guess the note from the haunted old garage must have had evil powers. Still, the shaky answer to my note, "Hello, Skeeter," didn't really strike me as evil, but as kind of lonely—the same loneliness I felt sitting out on our steps at night. But it turned my tears and anger against my friends. What right had they to come and use my tent without me, and to burn candles. I knew I'd never get another tent.

I wanted to talk to someone about the fire and the note, but couldn't think of anyone who would understand. I knew my family would say the destruction of my tent was no more than an unfortunate accident. If Mat heard about the note he'd insist I was the victim of a prank. Friends would think me crazy. But something or someone knew me by name, and I could hardly think what to do.

Finally I decided I could talk to Mr. Gerber, our church's youth and music minister. Mr. Gerber played basketball as agilely as the kids, and he could sing, too. He had a rich baritone voice, an athletic build, and was always ready to jump into action. Though he was beginning to acquire a bald dome, the rest of his head was thatched with thick kinky hair which merged with long sideburns into a dense black beard. I always had the feeling that his head would look exactly the same upside down.

He laughed a lot, and since my home did not indulge in much laughter I gravitated toward him. His wife was a plumpish woman who joined him in duets. Their two children, a boy and a girl, were both pupils at Wynnton.

I rode over to the church, leaned my bike against a big oak tree, and climbed the stairs to the second floor offices. Mrs. Franklin at the reception desk, busy on the phone, nodded to me, and off in the downstairs nursery I could hear a child crying. Mr. Gerber was in his office and invited me right in. He leaned back in his chair, his hands clasped behind his head, and motioned for me to sit down. "Well, Skeeter, to what do I owe this honor?"

Half-stammering, I told him about the note and the haunted garage.

He listened without interrupting. "Do you really think an evil spirit could write you a note?"

"All I know is that place is black and smelly and spooky. Nobody ever goes in there. I guess you just think I'm imagining things."

"Maybe, maybe not. I believe there are paranormal events we can't explain. Is there anything else?"

I told him about seeing the attic curtain drop when nobody was supposed to be upstairs, about the body parts, about Russell's baby sister being kidnapped, about my tent burning down. "And that note, the one I hid in my tent. Maybe that's why it caught fire …"

Mr. Gerber leaned further back in his chair. "Skeeter, I must tell you, I think anyone who wrote you a note was certainly human."

"Maybe half human."

"I have no doubt that evil dwells among us, but I happen to believe in the long run good wins out."

"But first you have to believe the things you've been taught are really true."

A look of sympathy crossed his face. "Sometimes we have doubts. We're afraid our hopes and expectations will pass us by. But I think you're too young to worry about missing out."

The phone rang and I started to get up but he motioned me to remain seated. I listened as he exchanged a few casual remarks with Mrs. Gerber. I'd once heard a couple of the older boys snicker, "Mr. Gerber's a lady's man." But his voice was kind and affectionate.

I remembered seeing Mrs. Gerber once in Kirven's Department Store. I started over to speak to her, but was stopped by a look on her face, an expression of frustration. She stood before a mirror, holding a dress to her shoulders. She was a stout woman. She jerked the dress away, and I felt pity for her. She must think herself unattractive. At church, though, she always seemed happy.

We talked a while longer and when it was time for me to leave, Mr. Gerber said, "Come back anytime, Skeeter. Really. I enjoy talking to you."

As I rode away I felt I hadn't accomplished much, but just talking did seem to help a little. I couldn't get over the destruction of my tent from which I had received so much pleasure and which was the one place I could truly call my own.

I decided to go back to see Mr. Gerber on Friday. Most of the staff were off, and the building was quiet, only a few lights burning here and there. I entered through a side door, passed down a short flight of steps, and made my way through the downstairs fellowship hall. There were the odors of dried flowers and janitor's supplies, of waxed tile and Wednesday's family night cooking.

At the end of the fellowship hall I climbed a double flight of stairs to reach the upper level and the corridor of offices behind the sanctuary. Here were many doors—to the baptistery, the choir loft, the sanctuary balcony, the church offices, the stairways. I knew them all and went straight to Mr. Gerber's office. There appeared to be no one else in the building. Mr. Gerber's door was open, the lights on, but he wasn't inside. As I turned to leave I heard the muffled laugh of a woman, and it seemed to be originating in the choir room on the opposite side of the baptistery. I made my way around. The door was cracked a little, and I had just raised my arm to knock or nudge it open when through the narrow crack I saw Mr. Gerber and a young woman who was a member of the choir.

They were standing together, kissing. A shock went through me. He was married, a minister, and here he was kissing a woman who was not his wife.

Dizzy with anger and disillusion, I wanted to crash open the door and scream, "Liar! Liar!" Instead I turned and fled, blinded by disgust. Possibly the echo of my retreating footfalls halted them, possibly this was their one single slip. I had no way of knowing. The image I had of Mr. Gerber was forever tarnished. I felt sorry for Mrs. Gerber and the children, too, realizing that if she had any idea what sort of things her husband was doing she must feel terrible.

On my bike I flew home, never wanting to see Mr. Gerber again. Almost instantly I began to wonder what good it did to go to church. The Parises never went, neither did the Quinceys. How was my family different from theirs? If everybody acted alike, if everybody wanted the same things, what exactly was the special promise belief was supposed to give? It all seemed like a colossal lie.

For the next two Sundays I faked a queasy stomach and skipped church. My Mother began to suspect something so finally I had to go back. When Mr. Gerber led the singing I refused to follow him and looked down at my book. Once I glanced up at Mrs. Gerber in the choir and saw that she was faking, too—smiling as though there was nothing else she'd rather be doing.

Not long afterward Mr. Gerber resigned and moved away. All the kids were sorry to see him go. I thought about the things he'd taught us as our youth minister. Talk was cheap, I knew, it was the way people acted that mattered.

Actions speak louder than words.

* * *

Pudge Brewster, a friend of Mat's, stood with his back against our living room mantle, toasting his behind over our small radiant heater. "Listen to this, Skeeter." He looked at me, then turned a few pages of a paperback novel. "The worst of all is the neck because the head is gone and the neck spurts blood for a little bit while the heart doesn't know its vital nerve center is gone — and do you know how high the blood can spurt? No! Then let me tell you."

He slapped the novel shut. "What do you think?"

"I don't know," I said.

"Mickey Spillane. A hot new writer. Gets fifty grand a book."

"It sounds kind of gruesome."

"Gruesome's in," said Pudge. He read a few more passages and they made me queasy and fascinated. When he and Mat went out he left the novel on the mantle. I picked it up and began reading. Mama said, "Put that down. You don't need to read that trash, Skeeter."

"How do you know it's trash? Have you read it?'

"I've read about him."

"I bet Mat reads it."

"Mat's six years older than you. He doesn't need to read it, either."

My interest had only been casual, but now that I was warned it became intense. But out of respect for her I put the book aside and a while later Pudge came back by to retrieve it. "I don't see why I can't read anything," I complained.

"You wouldn't understand," said Mama. "That's meant for older minds. Sick minds."

"Is it sick minds who pay him all that money?"

"I hate to see a son of mine thinking like this."

What Mama didn't realize was that the comic books kids passed around were no less brutal than Mickey Spillane. Pokers were used to brand disloyal girls, girls plunged ice picks into the eyes of enemies, corpses were strung up by their genitals — it was all depicted in colorful detail in the comics. Mostly I avoided these because I wanted to sleep at night.

"If you want to read, read the book your teacher gave you. How far have you gone?"

My silence confessed I hadn't read *Remi.*

"I think Miss Barton would be very disappointed."

Actually, I had an idea Mama did read Spillane sometimes, because she read everything. She always had a book in her hand, and though her formal education was limited, she'd learned a great deal about life through the books she read. Given the opportunity, she might have excelled beyond our little house on Schaul, but she never complained, and her great ambition now was to see us children do well.

I had no further opportunity to read Mickey Spillane but I wondered what it was like to have fifty thousand dollars. It seemed to me our neighbors all up and down the street were better off than we were—not much, but enough to make a difference. I tried hard not to compare what we had with what they had, for Miss Barton had given us another little gem of wisdom: *It is comparison that makes men miserable.*

* * *

For her birthday Mat's girlfriend Margaret Howell received a beautiful canary-yellow Cadillac convertible. It had belonged to her mother, who'd gotten a new one. The Caddy was just two years old, but before the keys were handed over to Margaret it was cleaned, waxed and shined bumper-to-bumper. Often it had swept up the Columbus High driveway to deliver Margaret to classes as Mrs. Howell sped away, top down, hair blowing. Students and faculty observed this ritual with envy or disdain, though Margaret herself had taken it all in stride, as rich girls often do, neither condescending nor haughty.

Her personal possession of the canary bird made a material difference. At first Mat, too, was happy to drive this snazzy machine. She tossed him the keys, snuggled up close and they squealed off. It increased his stature in the eyes of his peers and in his own eyes. But more intriguing to him was this power at his fingertips and his command of the rich majorette at his side. After a brief time, though, the convertible became a source of conflict between them. He declined to set foot in it, insisting instead that they take our old Chevy, even to a dance or some function they attended with Margaret all decked out.

When he took our car, Mat, much to his chagrin, frequently had to drop me off somewhere, and I became the hapless observer of their arguments. These were generally kept in check during my presence, but if they became heated the two of them forgot me in the back seat. When Margaret became fervent in her point of view, she moved a bit away, fixed him with a defiant stare, and emphasized every few words. "Why *can't* we take my car to the parade! Explain *that* to me, please!"

"Because I don't want to."

"Most boys would give *anything* to drive a convertible in a parade."

"Give them your keys, then. I don't have to show off in my girlfriend's car."

She didn't get it, but I did. Mat might be a bit jealous of the country club set, but he despised the pretense. It became hypocritical for him to drive his girlfriend's Cadillac for which he couldn't afford gas. Margaret on the other hand was accustomed to an unrestrained lifestyle and infatuated as she was with him she was too fond of society to renounce it. I couldn't have put such thoughts into words then, but I had begun to understand that rich boys and girls in time reached an age to begin to exercise their hierarchy, the nascent snobbery Mat had come to hate.

"Oh, I wish I didn't *have* the damn car!" Margaret cried.

"Give it back, then."

She looked aghast. "You *are* mad!"

To such confrontations I was frequently an unwilling party.

When the Columbus High marching band performed out of town, Mat insisted on riding not in the chartered bus but in his own car. Few of his friends were in the band but those who were felt the same way. They all wanted to play their trumpets and clarinets and take advantage of the opportunity to travel out of town with a girl. Mat was too independent to care much for the riotous bus rides with the singing and cheering, the chaperones and sleepy return trips home.

"My parents won't let me go with you," said Margaret.

"Why did you even ask?"

"They'll see that I get on that bus and they'll be *waiting* when we pull in."

"Okay, I'll follow and at the first rest stop you can get off the bus and hook up with me."

"And if something happens to your old car, if it breaks down or something happens to the bus, how long do you think it'll take them to find out?"

"You'd just tell them I was coming along and you didn't see anything wrong with it."

"Would you *really* deceive them if you thought we could get away with it?"

"Would you?"

"Yes," she said, "but that isn't the point. We might *not* get away with it, then there would be *hell* to pay."

"You could work something out," he said stubbornly.

"Even if I could, they'd just be *furious* with you."

"As if they didn't already want to break us up."

"I can assure you I've straightened them out on *that*."

I'd noticed something in Margaret I could hardly understand. Having accomplished her intent, she turned all sweet and mushy and put her head on his shoulder. "We'll work something out. You must understand that I can't *totally* disobey Mother and Daddy." She giggled. "Don't forget there's the matter of the dowry."

For every conflict I witnessed there were dozens I only gleaned through the expressions on Mat's face. I could always tell when he was passionately in love and when there had been serious disharmony between them. He became more taciturn and tense, and at home his responses were rebellious and abrupt.

I believed Margaret's family's social ambition for their daughter was bound to make her reject Mat as a long-term suitor. They might be willing to allow her liberty in flirtations if they could use these to indoctrinate her to the future she was really cut out for. The religiosity of prominent men and families was very public, they had great halls and buildings and chapels named after them, they poured money into charitable institutions and made themselves notable public servants, but the concept of throwing the doors of their homes open to the lost and impoverished was unthinkable.

But for Mat self-reliance was what he could see, touch, absorb, and this he plunged into with dogged determination. It was impossible that these social differences didn't surface from time to time, and I think this was what irritated Mat most and made him suffer most—the rich daughter and the poor suitor whose fiery chemistry was almost guaranteed to be self-destructive. It frightened me to see instinctively that he was playing with fire. I liked Margaret, she was always sweet to me, but I hated the way their relationship made him so miserable. I think Mat realized that Margaret's underlying expectations and his view of life were bound to crash. To her, love might have been blind. To him, it demanded strategic reckoning. But he was dead set against backing off.

"Why don't you get another girlfriend?" I once asked him. "You can have any girl you want."

This merely irritated him. Mat didn't really want to talk to me. He had no idea how deeply a frightened younger brother could desire a word of approval from an older. But I knew I would never get this. He had to tolerate me because we shared the same house and the same bedroom, but he couldn't give me the time of day. What I did to deserve his ire I was uncertain, but I reacted in kind—as much as possible I wanted him to stay clear of me and my friends.

As a small boy Mat had contracted malaria and almost died. His health was never fully restored, he was inclined to pick up viruses and was allergic to a number of medicines and antibiotics. His thin frame and delicate features had subjected him to a lifetime of harassment. His defense against these assaults had emerged in an indestructibility and tough cynicism that made him guard his own feelings and his own wants like a territorial lion. In this respect he and Margaret were too much alike: they both were self-centered.

Margaret, pretty, wild, headstrong, pampered, personified Columbus elitism and snobbery. Mat cared nothing for class and relied for his foundation on no special favors but on self-motivation and tough stoicism, virtues he had learned from the circumstances of want. So I knew his relations with Margaret were destined to crash, and as distanced as we were from one another, I was terrified to think what this would do to him.

8

I woke Saturday morning dreading the hours I would have to spend out on my route collecting for the paper. I knew the only way I could ever hope for a new bike or prepare for Daddy losing his job was to work hard and make money. With my tattered record book I started out early, trying to finish as soon as possible, but there were always complications and delays. There'd be no one home, change could not be found, I couldn't break a five dollar bill, a customer argued that he hadn't missed last week's payment. Those from whom I failed to collect on Saturday forced me to interrupt my deliveries the following week to knock on doors the second or third times.

Mr. Charles, a wealthy owner of a furniture store who lived on Wildwood Avenue, never paid. He would open his door with an etched scowl of irritation, frown wrinkles around his eyes, compressed lips, and a generous girth which he carried like a mantle of his wealth. While times were lean for so many, he could dine with pleasure at the town's finest clubs, and never failed to let his prowess be known.

"Collect for *The Ledger*, please."

"How much?" He always asked how much.

"Thirty-five cents."

"Well, I don't have it on me. Try next week."

Next week Mrs. Charles or one of their high school kids would say, "You can catch Mr. Charles at the store."

So if I wanted my thirty-five cents I'd have to ride three miles to the furniture store on lower Broad, and Mr. Charles, with a gesture of irritation, would slap it into my hands as though paying a ransom; yet, if he came home and found no paper waiting for him he'd be the first to call Circulation and complain.

When I finished collecting early enough, I hurried down to Chattahoochee Paint and Hardware to catch Daddy before lunch. I'd find him looking at paint swatches with a customer, or mixing paint, at which he was an expert — a squirt of burnt sienna, a dollop of raw umber to achieve a perfect match. He was good with hardware, too. With a glance he could tell you if a wrench was 7/16ths or 3/8ths. This Saturday he raised his hand to me and I drifted around the store. Chattahoochee wasn't nearly as diversified as William Beach where Daddy had worked during the war, but had established a niche with new electric tools and kitchen appliances, a nice toy department and a generous lay-away program.

As Daddy finished with his customer he motioned me over. "You ride your bike down here?"

"No, sir, I rode the bus."

"Good. Pretty cold for biking. You hungry?"

"Yes, sir."

"Let's get something to eat, then."

As we started out, Mr. Montgomery, standing in front of the store talking to some businessmen, said, "Hurry back, Nathan, we have a big batch of paint to mix for Monday."

"It's supposed to be too cold to paint Monday."

"You let me worry about that."

I saw the slightest expression of disgust flick across Daddy's face. Government specifications prohibited painting in temperatures lower than forty degrees, but by paying off the inspectors Mr. Montgomery was able to push his jobs through and take on more contracts.

As we hurried along I asked, "How long are you going to work for that man?"

95

"As long as he pays me, I guess."

"He should be working for you," I said.

This seemed to amuse him. "Why?"

"Because you're ten times better. A hundred." We walked up Broad, toward Eleventh. "You'd never cheat anybody."

"I hope you won't let on you know about that, Skeeter. I'd lose my job. And they aren't easy to find."

"Someday he'll get caught," I said. "People who do bad things always get caught."

"Not always," he said. "But you go right on believing that." He was silent a moment, then said, "People have to make the best of things."

"What would you change if you could?"

Another moment of silence. "I guess I'd like to open my own store."

"Why don't you?"

"It's a big risk. Maybe someday..."

Occasionally we would walk all the way up Broadway to the Orange Bowl which served hot sandwiches and wonderful fruit punch, or we would go to the Krystal. Today we walked to the pool hall which specialized in spicy hotdogs and grilled cheese sandwiches and BLT's. In back was the billiards parlor where fugitives from society hung out, men who drank beer and shot pool, lifting their eyes suspiciously to newcomers, and respected businessmen in suits who grabbed a half hour at noon to take out their tension on the sticks. The dim light, the odor of beer, the thick shrouds of cigarette smoke all seemed mysterious and clandestine to me; perhaps this was why Daddy seated himself on a stool to my right, shielding me from the semi-dark inner chamber.

We had sandwiches and root beer, then as we started back to the store I noticed that Daddy's step wasn't as brisk as it had been. I wished I could take away his troubles. I wished I understood why a man like Blaise Montgomery could have so much while my father struggled just to hold things together. I knew he was torn between the challenge to step forth with the truth or stay quiet and keep his job.

In front of Chattahoochee Paint Daddy said, "I'm glad you came, Skeeter. It breaks up the day."

* * *

Whether the evil of the old garage were inhuman or half human I didn't know, but it constantly reminded me of how much there was to fear in the world. I feared Daddy having no income, I feared the troubles my brother could get himself into, and more than anything else I feared that something could happen to mother or daddy.

I knew there was more than one way to lose a parent. One of my mother's brothers Uncle Brent was an alcoholic and when he went on a binge my cousins lost him. Closer to home was the Greshams who lived just across the street from us. Jean Gresham was a year younger than I and we were close neighborhood friends. But she was tormented by her mother whom Daddy uncharitably called a "dope fiend."

One Saturday I arrived home from collecting for the papers and was looking forward to free time when Mother shuffled Joanie out onto the porch and said, "Play with her a little while, Skeeter."

Much as I loved my little sister I wanted to hook up with Tommy or Malcolm and not get stuck with babysitting.

"Do I have to?"

"Just for a little while. It won't be long."

I caught a glimpse of Jean Gresham's mother in her nurse's uniform and the light dawned.

"It's Mrs. Gresham, isn't it?"

"Yes. Now go on, Skeeter, you don't need to be here."

I took Joanie by the hand and led her down the steps. She came willingly, always eager for attention and for getting outside. At the edge of our grassed yard was a gentle slope contoured down to the curb. She released my hand and for a few minutes amused herself walking up and down this slope, taking quick tottering steps and laughing. I sat on the curb imagining what was going on inside our house. I had been witness to unpleasant scenes in the past, and it irked me that Mrs. Gresham subjected Mama to them no matter how hard she tried to resist.

Straining my ears I could hear my mother implore, "You shouldn't do this, Lynda. You know it's wrong."

"Oh, but you don't understand!" cried Mrs. Gresham. "You don't *understand!*"

"I understand you're destroying yourself. And your daughter."

Joanie came up the little slope and handed me a rock she'd found in the grass. She then took it from me. It was great fun, this giving and taking away, and I could indulge her without much distraction. From inside I heard, "I'll make us some coffee. Maybe that'll calm you down."

"I don't want coffee! I want to use your bathroom!"

I knew this was just the beginning of a struggle that was bound to get worse, and as I sat on the steps half striving to hear, half wanting to run away, I became as tense as I knew Mother was. As long as things were going well, Mrs. Gresham was a sweet, thoughtful person. But when she needed a "fix" she became high strung, disoriented, and wild — a different, almost deranged woman. If she were watched too closely at home she slipped out and tormented my mother and other neighbors, dead set on using their bathrooms. I don't know what she needed, perhaps a little water, a little flame, a shelf or an arm rest. I only knew that when she came to our house pleading to use the bathroom she locked herself in for five or ten minutes and emerged a different person. "She's nothing but a dope fiend," Daddy said, to which my mother replied, "You never know what drives a person to do things."

It was funny in a pathetic sort of way that Schaul Street had its two marauders, both of whom were liked in their natural state, both of whom found doors closed when they began foraging for their particular brand of conspiracies: Mr. Quincey, who would literally stand on a porch and talk non-stop for an hour, and Mrs. Gresham who invaded relatively calm households with such disrupting desperation.

Mother exclaimed, "I don't want you doing that in my house, Lynda. Go somewhere else!"

"Somewhere else! Where is there to go!"

"Why do you think my children should see something you don't want your own child to see?"

"Oh, you are so cruel! So *cruel!*"

The more Mama resisted, the louder Mrs. Gresham became. She was a nurse, and a good one, we understood. She lived with Jean and her own mother. When Jean and the grandmother were absent she could do as she pleased, but under their strict scrutiny her habits had to go underground. All the neighborhood accepted Mrs. Gresham when she was her calm self, but guarded their doors when she approached with a nervous, high-strung, intent gait. Rumor had it that she'd gotten hooked during the war when doctors and nurses resorted to drugs to escape the pressures.

"Look at me!" cried Mrs. Gresham suddenly. "Don't you see I can't help this! Oh, please, please, just leave me alone for ten minutes!"

"This is our home!" Mama cried just as loudly. "How dare you defile it like this!"

"Is that all you can think about! Yourself! You wouldn't treat a dog this way!"

Hearing the anguish in Mrs. Gresham's voice, I felt sorry for her. But I knew Mama hated the abuse of alcohol and drugs and thought of this as a vile dirty habit, not an illness. Noticing that Joanie had suddenly paused and stood listening, not so much to the words as to the tone in Mama's voice, I jumped up and took her hand. "C'mon, Joanie, we'll go for a walk."

No sooner had I led Joanie from the yard than I saw Jean Gresham come out onto her front steps and sink down. She looked toward Joanie and me but didn't wave. A sharp pang of pity swept through me. I knew Jean was in pain. Her father had abandoned them when she was an infant, she'd relied more or less on her grandmother to nurture her, and here was her mother hooked on something neither of us fully understood, something which made her so disoriented and wild all maternal instincts were cast to the wind. In my heart I prayed that I would never lose my mother or father in such a way or in an accident or sickness.

I took Joanie across the street and sat down beside Jean. Without a word of greeting she said, "My mother's sick." She sat quite still, her arms around her knees, her head bowed.

I didn't respond, knowing her mother was putting my mother under great stress and resenting it.

Still without looking at me she muttered, "I'm sorry, Skeeter." She sounded lonely and helpless.

"It's okay."

"Please don't hate her. Or me."

"I don't hate anybody."

"She's sick. Sometimes I wonder if she's ever tried to get over it. She humiliates me. She humiliates herself. Something's got control of her she can't change."

"Are you scared sometimes?"

"Yes, I'm scared."

"Me, too."

She turned to look at me. Without her glasses her eyes had a special kind of depth and luminosity.

"Why are you afraid?" she asked.

"I don't know. Things … make me."

"I think mostly we make ourselves afraid. I know when I start thinking I get scared. The things that've happened. The things that might happen. Things I want and don't want. I'm scared of myself sometimes."

"But I don't know if you can make yourself stop being afraid."

"Maybe you can stop thinking about things that make you different from the way you want to be."

This sounded like someone much older, and I was sorry Jean was having to grow up too fast, without a father. Sometimes I was growing up too fast, too.

She said distractedly, "Look at Joanie. She doesn't look much like you, Skeeter. Who does she favor?"

"I don't know. My daddy, I guess."

"You and Mat look alike."

This was a compliment, I always thought Mat much better looking than I. "There's your mom," I said.

Mrs. Gresham came out of our house, apparently having gotten her way as usual. I could tell by the way she walked—balanced, purposeful, her head high. She no doubt had worn Mama down, used our bathroom, locked the door and pulled a needle, a substance, perhaps a candle, whatever she needed from her purse. The transformation was swift. Jean watched her with both sadness and relief. They'd have a little time again when they could be mother and daughter, but everyone knew the demon would haunt their lives and eat at them like a cancer.

As Joanie began tugging at me to get up, I stood and looked down at Jean who sat watching her mother. "I'm glad your Mama's feeling better now."

She turned her eyes up to me. "I have a good mother," she said. "She'll do anything for me."

"I know. You for her, too."

I took Joanie's hand and hurried away, not wanting to witness their pitiful reunion, with another kind of fear shivering through me.

* * *

Daddy skulked off to work each morning never knowing when his crooked boss would let him go and struggling to make the best of his day. Mama was an accomplished seamstress and picked up a few dollars sewing for others. She underestimated herself and never thought her work good enough to charge very much for. She never accepted payment from relatives and neighbors and almost never sewed for anyone she didn't know; but occasionally she'd accept a job when no one else could be found.

I was in the driveway working on my bike when a spectacular Buick pulled up to the curb in front of our house. It was glistening white and long as a hearse. The well-heeled lady who got out was just as spectacular, with necklaces of various lengths on her plump bodice, rings on nearly every finger and bracelets jangling on her wrists beneath the sleeves of her coat. The coat, with a luxurious fur collar, made her look hot, and one could scarcely doubt that she wore it for show, not warmth. She nodded to me and I ran to open the door.

"Mrs. Sterling's here."

"Well, the dress is ready, I think," Mama said.

Mrs. Sterling had brought Mama a striking pale pink evening gown which had to be modified for her daughter's upcoming Country Club dance. It was loose in the shoulders and waist, the straps had to be removed and resewn and nearly all the seams trimmed down. Mama was such a perfectionist that if she discovered one dropped stitch she'd rip out the entire seam and start over. She had labored until late night hours on this gown after Mrs. Sterling had insisted that she'd been able to find no one else who'd do it.

Mama brought out the dress on a hanger. "Is your daughter with you? I'd like to see it on her."

Mrs. Sterling examined the gown from every angle. "Oh, you know how these girls are. Too busy for anything. I'm just picking it up for her."

She opened her purse and pulled out a ten and a five dollar bill previously folded together in a side pocket. "Fifteen dollars, as I recall."

Mama hesitated. "I believe we agreed on twenty."

"I'm certain it was fifteen."

I had been in the room when the arrangements made, and wanted to shout, "It was twenty dollars!" But of course I said nothing.

"Well, all right," Mama said. "If that's the way you remember it."

Mrs. Sterling closed her purse, took the dress and went out. As she drove away I cried, "Why did you let her do that? She knew it was twenty dollars!"

"Maybe she lost track."

"She cheated you, that's all! She just deliberately cheated you."

Mama was the most forgiving person in the world, but it irritated me to see her let people get by with such things. No matter what anybody did to her she always found some excuse for them.

Angrily, I said, "I hope you never sew for her again."

To this she didn't respond. She was looking at the fifteen dollars and probably thinking that at least this could pay something on our medical bill.

"You won't, will you?"

"No, I guess not," she said at last.

It was just about impossible not to wonder why God let us suffer so when the Montgomerys and Sterlings led their lives with such careless greed.

God was a subject about whom I'd had several arguments with Pudge Brewster, who'd tried to introduce me to Mickey Spillane, and who enjoyed nothing more than taunting me.

"It's a dog eat dog world," said Pudge. "God is just something people invented who want to believe they'll live forever."

"That's not all it means. It's something inside, too. It's helping others."

"Ha! Animals help others. Elephants. Gorillas. Your ancestors were monkeys."

"No, yours were. Or skunks."

"You came from a single-cell amoeba. A black dark nothing. You evolved into a *Homo sapiens*."

"Why don't we keep going then? Why did we stop evolving?"

"Because we reached the top of the food chain. Evolution ends with the survival of the fittest."

Pudge didn't believe half the things he said, but he wanted to get a rise out of me.

"Listen, Skeeter, all people care about is *things*. Things that make them rich and alive. Someday, this country will be too wealthy to need heaven."

"I hope I'm never that wealthy."

"You may change your mind as you grow up."

While Pudge Brewster played the devil's advocate, trying to rile me, the only boy I knew who was an avowed atheist was in sixth grade at Wynnton. His name was Claude Zucesulli. He was older, taller, and had it in for me either because of the special favors I received from Jack, warming myself in the furnace room while he, Claude, froze on the grounds, or because he truly hated my religion. I knew he wanted to goad me into a fight, but I didn't intend to be like my brother; I thought fighting cheap and stupid. Even so, when Claude said those who believed in God were merely "Neanderthals" and "simpletons" I wanted to grind his face into the ground.

"People believe what they're taught," Claude said. "If you were taught frogs had magical powers you'd believe it. If you were taught Oak Mountain could transform your life you'd believe that."

Claude Zucesulli had sallow skin and a pockmarked face. He wheezed and made little attempt to tame his hair which grew in ragged spurts on the front and back of his skull. I was afraid of him but not as afraid as I had been of Joe Turner. Somehow I could return Claude's contempt with such fierce loyalty to my beliefs it was as if something bigger than I provided courage.

Finally, though, Claude found an opportunity to attack me. We were on the playground engaged in a softball game. I was never very good at sports, always the last to be chosen when teams sided up. I missed an easy fly ball to centerfield and our team lost the inning. From second base Claude cursed me and I retaliated by telling him he looked like a corpse. I saw him coming, murder in his eyes. Without a word of warning he swung a big looping fist at my chin. I was able to turn my shoulders enough to take the blow on the neck. Before he threw a second blow I ducked my head and began to flail wildly, neither knowing nor caring what I hit but knowing from the solid connections with flesh and bone that I must be inflicting damage.

I could scarcely believe I was in a fight. It was my first. I thought it inexcusable, and knew I was getting whipped. I wondered in the bitter dark canyons of my mind if this was retribution I deserved. I fell to my knees and a boy trying to scrabble away stepped on the middle finger of my left hand. My fingernail was crushed. I jumped to my feet and started swinging again. There was only one reason I could think of that prevented my running away. I wanted to disembowel Claude, I wanted him to feel punishment, to know pain as I knew it. The bell rang and the fight broke up, several boys pushing us away from each other and dragging us by the arms toward class. Demoralized, with hands, nose and eyes burning, I let myself be hustled along, embarrassingly defeated.

"Good fight, Skeeter," one of the boys said. "You got in your licks."

"He beat me," I mumbled.

"No, he didn't. He took as much as he gave."

This surprised me and pumped me up a little. But I was ashamed. Word of the fight preceded us into the classrooms and as I walked in Miss Barton looked at me with disdain.

"Brawling like two savages," she said.

I dropped my chin. "He started it."

"What does it matter who started it? This is beneath you, Skeeter."

Defensively, I mumbled, "I don't like fighting."

Still her glare drilled into me. "Actions speak louder than words"—one of her oft-repeated proverbs. "These are not frivolous sayings, Skeeter. They're meant to enlighten you."

"Yes, ma'am."

"Keep your arms at your side." The second time I'd heard this.

I nodded obediently, but for all these wonderful maxims I reckoned it was my fists which taught Claude Zucesulli to leave me alone. After that we still found ourselves on the field together, but he seldom spoke to me. Still, I could not help but notice, as we left school that afternoon, my own nose and ears stinging, that it was Claude the atheist, not I, who rode away on a sleek wine-red Schwinn.

9

My note—"I'm not afraid of you!" and its perplexing answer—"Hello, Skeeter"—had gone up in flames with my tent, and I couldn't prove it ever existed even if I wanted to, and I didn't want to. At one moment I was tormented by the "Hello, Skeeter," as though this evil spirit knew me by name, and the next by an almost shy "Hello, Skeeter ..." as if something were reaching out to me. In which should I believe? Not knowing was as frightening as imagining the worst.

The scary part was that I felt drawn to the old garage as a moth is drawn to flame. I knew I should let it go, but couldn't. Malcolm suggested that I should write another note.

"What would I say?"

"Don't ask me. I don't want to be a part of it. But you're all tied in now."

I wondered what would be of significance to whoever or whatever prowled this dank, lightless grave? Maybe, "Leave me alone!" At last, on school tablet paper, I wrote, "Do you like darkness or sunshine best?"

Again I chose a bright afternoon, cold but flooded with sunlight. I parked my bike well away and checked to see who was about. Down on the corner of Marian and Henry a plumpish woman stood waiting for the bus. Up the street a couple of men in painter's overalls, notebooks and pencils in hand, were walking around a house. Witnesses and rescuers were within hailing distance should I encounter trouble.

This time instead of inserting my note halfway through the crack in the doors, I thrust it hard forward, letting it fall well into the padlocked garage. I then ran back to my bicycle and hurried away. For the next three days I passed the garage going to and coming back from school and my paper route, and each time as I drew close I tensed with anticipation. But there was no evidence that my note didn't lie decaying on the dirt floor, soaking up grime and moisture and possibly gnawed by rats.

Then as I hurried home from school on Friday I caught a glimpse of something white. My heart leaped and I had to decide whether to run away or find out if this was my answer. Finally I mustered courage to run up to the doors, grab the paper and flee as quickly as possible.

With trembling hand I unfolded the note. It was my own tablet paper and my own writing all right. "Do you like darkness or sunshine best?" Beneath my firm but slightly unsteady script was the same neat delicate hand I'd seen before. It said, as though it understood my meaning, "Sunshine's better for you."

I anguished over this response. Sunshine is better for me personally? Did he or it really know me? Or better for all boys? Did it mean that only bright light could protect me from the black threat of the decaying garage?

No doubt I'd only made matters worse. No one should dialogue with the devil. Yet, I was gripped by a conspiratorial spirit which held me in a kind of terrified awe.

* * *

Daddy arrived home with the guarded glance and hunched shoulders we were seeing more and more lately. Some man in plain business attire had come into the store to prowl around, and Daddy suspected he was an investigator with the Provost Marshall's office or with Army Intelligence.

"I think maybe they've got wind of something. They talked mostly to the boys in the paint department."

"You think they know what's going on?" asked Mama.

"Maybe."

"I wish *you* didn't know."

Seldom did we see a visual manifestation of the emotions Daddy was going through. He held his feelings silently, hardly ever expressing anxiety or affection, but worry now was etched into the fine lines of his forehead.

"What did you tell the investigator?" Mother asked.

"Dodged as best I could. Told him I dealt mostly with hardware." He reflected solemnly, "It's the devil to be in a trap." Still, when he went out to get his tools we heard him whistling. I never knew if this whistling was a way to release tension or if he really was able to put the day's turmoil behind. I'm sure it didn't make him feel better that just as he went out Mama said, "I know about being in a trap." She looked at Joanie and me. "They know, too."

I was sorry she said this. I thought Daddy was doing everything he could under the circumstances. Almost every night he left after supper to some side job even in the most brutal weather. Tonight seemed particularly forbidding and I grabbed my jacket and cap and ran after him. "I'll go help."

He shook his head. "I don't know that you could do very much, Skeeter."

"If I can throw papers, I can help you."

"That's a point, I guess."

I helped put the tools in the trunk and we drove out of town. Right away dread came over me. The temperature was plunging, the place we were going was far out in the country. For an hour we drove up and down roads asking directions but were unable to find the place. "We're losing a lot of time," said Daddy.

"Will this be our only job tonight?"

"It'll have to be."

Finally we pulled into a long sweeping driveway lined with great magnolia trees, at the end of which stood a country mansion. "I think this is it," Daddy said.

"Wow, they're rich!" I exclaimed.

"I don't imagine they miss any meals."

As we got out a cutting slice of cold hit us. We knocked on a double white door with a large horseshoe-shaped knocker, and felt a new puff of cold as the door swung open. "Well, thank goodness! I was afraid you weren't coming!" A large, husky man wearing a fur-lined overcoat looked like a black bear with just his nose and gray eyes showing.

Behind him a woman, also wearing a coat, exclaimed, "I hope you can fix this thing! It's like a freezer in here."

"What can you tell me about it?"

"Nothing much. The heat went off as if there were no gas. But I just had the tank filled." He led us by flashlight out into the back of the big house where there was a bullet-shaped butane gas tank half hidden by cedar trees.

"Your valve still open?" asked Daddy.

"I closed it this morning. You can't smell this damn stuff, and I didn't want to take any chances." He showed us the scuttle under the house, then hurried back inside.

As I held our light, Daddy checked the valve, the fittings and the supply line to the ground. His fingertips were blue from cold, and my own nose and ears were stinging. On the hillside the unbroken wind was like rivets of ice. "Hope it's not a line broken underground," he said. "That could take all night."

Now that we'd spent so long finding the place, I thought about how late it was and about school tomorrow.

"I'll check under the house, Skeeter. You can go back to the car if you want to."

"I'll go with you. I came to help."

We opened the access door, dropped onto our knees and crawled under the big house. The ground was frozen and wet, smelling of dirt and mold, and there was so little head room we had to remain on all fours. Daddy located the supply lines where they rose from the ground and branched off to the furnaces. As I crawled beside him, he traced the lines and finally at one of the turns discovered a ruptured connection. "Here's where they're losing their supply, I think. Good thing he turned off the tank." With his light he showed me the broken fitting.

"What do you think happened?"

"Don't know. Sometimes things work loose all on their own."

From his tool pouch he extracted pliers and wrenches, and blowing on his fingers to make them a little more flexible, began to loosen the connections. "I'll need my flaring set, Skeeter. Think you can get it?"

"I know right where it is."

He shined the light across the cold crawl space. "There's the door. I'll need to keep the light."

"That's okay, I can see." I crawled out, stood shivering, then hurried to the car. The night was black, a scattering of stars providing no light at all, and all I could hear were crickets and deep-throated bullfrogs off on a pond far away. I wished more than anything to be back home warming my feet by our little space heater. I wished just as hard that Daddy didn't have to do this for extra money. I found the flaring set and made my way back under the old house. Daddy had the broken connection loose and in a few minutes he reflared the line and made up a new one. All the time he talked, explaining to me what he was doing, hunched over on his knees or sitting splay-legged on the ground.

"This is hard work," I said. "Dirty, too."

"Yes, it is." He tightened the fittings and carefully reboxed the flaring set. "We'll check the damper, too, while we're here."

We crawled over to the furnaces and examined the dampers. One of them was stuck, and in using his hands and pliers to adjust it he sliced his finger. Blood oozed out, eerie red in the dimming flashlight.

"Oh, Daddy!" I said.

"It's all right. No big thing."

From his pouch he extracted a sliver of cloth which didn't look very clean, wrapped it around his finger and crept back to the repaired connection. "Skeeter, if you could go out and open the valve I'll check this for leaks, then we're done."

I hurried across the yard, opened the valve, then stuck my head back through the scuttle. "It's open."

"Okay, everything looks all right here."

We gathered the tools and hastened back to the car. As the half-frozen grass crunched beneath my feet another surge of sadness came over me thinking of Daddy having to work like this night after night, especially in the freezing cold. We threw the pouch into the trunk and he removed the strip of cloth from his finger. "Skeeter, why don't you go tell Mr. Moultrie he can light his furnaces now. And he'll pay you. How much do you think we should charge?"

"I don't know. It's a long way out here."

"It is that, all right."

"And gas is expensive."

"So what do you think? Twelve dollars? Fifteen?"

I ran back to the porch where a big hanging brass fixture threw a warm light over everything. When Mr. Moultrie came to the door, still wearing his coat, I informed him about the furnaces. "You can turn up your heat now."

"Good. Thank you. Where's your dad?"

"Putting a bandage on his finger. He asked me to come tell you."

"He all right? He need help?"

"No, sir. He said you could pay me if you don't mind."

"Glad to. How much do I owe?"

"Twenty dollars," I said, "if that's not too much."

"Son, to get us heat in this house nothing's too much." He pulled a twenty and a five from his wallet. "Take this, and tell your father thanks very much."

"Thank you!" Mrs. Moultrie called from behind.

By the time I got back Daddy had started the car and turned on the heater. I jumped into the seat beside him, slammed the door, and pointed my toes toward the whir of heat. As I handed him the money, he looked at the bills. "What did you tell him?"

"Twenty dollars."

"Twenty dollars, huh." He grinned. "Maybe I better bring you along every time." He tried to give me the five but I refused.

"That's hard work," I said. "I just hate to see you have to do it."

He sighed and I realized how tired he really was. "We do what we have to, Skeeter. Maybe things'll be a little better for you."

By the time we drove home I could hardly hold my eyes open. I wondered how Daddy could keep going like this. I hoped his hand wouldn't become infected, and that his own chilled bones would find rest. I wondered if I could get another job and do more than just my paper route. I was full of all kinds of expectations and fears, but I felt very grown. I knew somehow someday I must do something to free Mama and Daddy from their prison.

But I remembered one of Miss Barton's favorite proverbs, one I would have to remind myself of all through life. *Don't bite off more than you can chew.*

10

Each morning I lay in bed waiting for Daddy, then Mat, to emerge from our bathroom so I could get ready for school. In the stillness outside, sounds were amplified. A milk truck went by, metal crates rattling, the clinking of bottles like sounds tapped on the windowpane. Squawking blue jays in the mimosas clattered across the roof like acorns falling. I wondered if all up and down Schaul Street people led lives as complicated as ours. What was going on behind the white porches of the Willises? The Joneses? The Neals?

One school day I remained home with a low-grade fever and nausea. All morning I took aspirin and Kool-Aid, bracing for my papers which had to be delivered no matter what. Tiring of bed I finally dressed and walked out to the street where with chalk I began to write little messages on the asphalt to various people—Malcolm, Tommy, Jean. All the other kids were in school, the street was practically deserted.

A young woman came along pulling her baby in a little red wagon. She was plain-looking, thin, with a long face and an unhappy expression. I raised my arm to wave and she waved back, then stopped to observe my proceedings.

"We used to write secret notes," she said, "and leave them in chewing gum wrappers."

This intrigued me. I stood to look closer at her.

"We'd take out the gum then fold little notes and slip them into the wrappers. Sooner or later someone would come along and find them."

"How did they know to look?"

"Oh, it was a well-known communication among us kids."

This seemed to me a wonderful new idea for covert communication and instantly I resolved to make use of it.

"That was a long time ago," she murmured quietly.

Her searching eyes and her gestures confused me. In one moment she looked caged and beaten, in the next her expression was hopeful and even content, especially when she glanced down at her baby. Her manner was kind, and I felt an instinctive liking for her.

"You live in that house," I said, pointing.

"Yes. Some."

"We play on your porch. When it's raining."

"I know."

I wondered if she realized she was the subject of yet another neighborhood scandal. We knew little about her other than that she was "that woman" who sometimes lived with Mr. Quincey. No one was certain whether the baby was his child, whether he'd just taken them both in or what their relations really were. Mr. Quincey no longer lived in town but kept the big house with its surrounding porch for his occasional return to Schaul Street. Some insisted he did this to goad Mrs. Quincey, his ex-wife, who lived directly across the street, and with whom he never ceased battle. This girl, and indeed to me she seemed no more than a girl, seldom showed her face except on days like this when the streets were deserted and she was unlikely to encounter anyone. Once or twice I'd caught a glimpse of Mr. Quincey going by in his pickup, with her and her baby sitting at his side. Mostly, though, he spirited her in and out, and she remained secluded as he ran around the neighborhood collecting rent and engaging anyone he could in long, rambling conversations.

I asked, "Are you going to stay here a while?"

"I don't know. If he lets me." I realized she must know that people talked about her. She leaned down to tuck the baby in and as she lifted her head she gave me one brief glance which I thought was uncertain and defenseless. I wondered if Mr. Quincey brightened her day or was cold to her, if he made demands, was generous or stingy. I knew she couldn't be content in her situation, particularly when he brought her here to taunt Mrs. Quincey who must have been at least twenty years older. I pitied her, she looked so pathetic and dazed.

"I have to go now," she said. "Don't forget the gum wrappers."

"I won't. Thanks." I stood silent as she pulled the wagon on up the street. I had neither asked her name nor given her mine.

Only one other time after that did I see this strange woman with her baby. This was one afternoon when Mr. Quincey's truck pulled up in front of the big house while Mrs. Quincey, his ex, happened to be out in her front yard, directly across the street. None of us who were out on Schaul at that time heard who said what first, but we soon were witness to an altercation between Mr. and Mrs. Quincey. He stood well away, not far from his truck, she in her yard, hands on her hips. As they argued back and forth the venom and volume increased. Neither tried to control their voices, their shouts held a ragged biting edge as they engaged in berating one another. The young woman, struggling to get her baby and bag out of the truck and into the house as quickly as possible, had not quite succeeded in vanishing when Mrs. Quincey cried, "You and your child whore!" and Mr. Quincey retorted just as loudly, "She can live a hundred years and never be a bitch like you!" At last one of the neighbors, Mr. Minor I think, came out of his house and stood glaring at them. This broke it up. Mr. Quincey retreated to his truck, Mrs. Quincey to her house.

I guess the reason I felt such pity for this girl was because I happened to be looking at her when Mrs. Quincey called her a whore, and she actually appeared to duck as if struck. Within weeks the neighborhood was saying, "Poor girl, she didn't realize what a sugar Daddy would cost her." And, "Wonder who the baby *really* looks like?"

When this sad situation turned into tragedy I wished I had at least learned the woman's name, that I had swallowed my shyness that day and been friendlier. Nobody knew what happened, but speculation was that either Mr. Quincey threw her out or he wanted her to stay, but she could no longer live under her circumstances. Nor did we know how she got down to the river. Perhaps Mr. Quincey dropped her off for some downtown shopping and she walked. It could have been something she planned or decided at the last instant.

She took her baby into her arms and walked out onto Dillingham Street Bridge, with its beautiful sweeping arches resembling some bridges in Europe. South of the Dillingham were rocky shoals and white rapids. The undercurrents beneath were said to be powerful and dangerous. Car traffic passed in one lane each way, and paralleling either lane were sidewalks for pedestrians and bicycles.

Witnesses said the young woman walked slowly out into the middle of the Dillingham and stood, baby in arms, looking pensively down at the water. No one thought anything about it, people often viewed the river from those vistas. Then slowly and deliberately she raised the baby to her lips, kissed it on both cheeks, reached out her arms and dropped the baby into the river. She leaned over, peering intently, as if to satisfy herself that the swift current had swallowed up the little blanket and baby romper. She then climbed up onto the banister, looked down again as though to confirm her intention, and threw herself into the current. A couple of boys fishing from the shoals below said not once did the baby or young woman surface. The undertow sucked them up and they were not found until two days later, a couple of miles down river. When I heard about this and remembered the look in the young woman's face, I cried myself to sleep.

For a long time after that we saw nothing of Mr. Quincey. When he did come around again, he skulked up and down the street engaging in his usual garrulous ramblings.

This was the second incident involving an innocent child within blocks of the evil old garage, and the murder-suicide struck renewed fear in my heart. It made me wonder just what it was that God is supposed to protect us from. This girl throwing herself and her baby to their deaths took my breath away. Maybe she believed that when she passed through the veil of cold water she would enter some new life. Maybe she could see something quite apart from the world which I was as yet unable to see. *God makes a nest for the blind bird.* I guess this was supposed to give me hope, but I wondered just how much of these feel-good promises could really be counted on.

* * *

If Daddy lost his job, the money I made throwing papers wouldn't go far but I thought even a little would help. So when our route manager Mr. Layfield called me down I was embarrassed, ashamed, and guilty.

"How many extras you carrying, Skeeter?" he asked.

"I don't know."

"Of course you do. How many?"

"About ten."

"Why don't you turn in drop slips?"

"I was going to."

He looked at me sternly. "When a customer moves away or cancels his subscription you should drop them. Why pay for papers you trash?"

I couldn't answer. I knew he was right. Normally I was so efficient and frugal I could not explain why I'd failed to write drop slips on ten papers I paid for unnecessarily.

"It's up to you, if you want to waste your money."

I knew Mr. Layfield had my best interest at heart. His own commission was based on the number of papers he distributed. He was a tall, slim man with thinning, amber-colored hair and a neat mustache. His eyes were washed-out gray from looking through dingy windshields, and his biceps disproportionately muscular from handling hundreds of stacks of bundled papers. His habit was to pull up to the school porch, drop off our wired bundles of *The Ledger*, and speed off. He went out of his way to have this conversation with me.

"I'm sorry, Mr. Layfield, I'll get the drop slips in."

"Not all at once, though. Two or three a week. We can't have a carrier dropping ten customers at once."

With this scolding from my manager, I felt myself to be living under constant stress. I needed to let off steam. So one Saturday when I finished collecting and was riding back home I hardly hesitated when two of my co-carriers, who were also students at Wynnton, contrived to invade the school's hallowed ground.

"C'mon, Skeeter, let's have some fun."

"I don't know. We could get caught."

"Right. So c'mon."

We hid our bikes, scaled the wrought-iron gates and were in the locked school grounds which were as deserted and silent as an old mining town. With shouts of glee we ran down the outside corridors, executed daredevil acrobatics on the slides and swings, and hoped some cop or parent would yell at us from beyond the fence so we could make a perilous escape like fleeing convicts. One of the boys skipped down the icy outside corridor banging on each classroom door and shouting an ugly word. His profanity echoed around the stuccoed walls of the buildings, and though I didn't hate school, his defamation was executed with such relish I couldn't resist some degree of conspiratorial rebellion. We ran around the little red brick building, the oldest school building in continuous operation in Georgia, which had sent forth scribes and Pharisees to Harvard, Yale, Radcliffe and Stanford and many other top colleges since 1843. Our worst offense was chalking words and drawings on the concrete corridor floors which could easily be washed off, though causing extra unnecessary work for Jack.

Nobody came to rout us, we were relieved and disappointed, and after an hour or so we jumped back over the gates, retrieved our bikes and went our separate ways. This sort of clandestine escape was about the extent of our criminality and was a brief release of tension for me, though I knew it wouldn't change anything.

* * *

The minute I walked into the classroom Miss Barton said, "Skeeter, go find Jack and ask him to come at once."

I could see why she wanted the janitor. It was about as icy in the room as it had been out at Mr. Moultrie's rural house, and the second time I had been involved with unworking heaters. Miss Barton's cheeks were rosy from the cold, her sturdy walking shoes fringed with frost. Elated that the teacher had chosen me, I ran to fetch Jack. As attuned as I now was to the soot-encrusted bowels of the basement I could almost hear the scraping of Jack's big coal shovel across the blackened concrete floor, feel the roaring flame as he pitched in coal, hear the clanging of the furnace doors and smell the ashes that he extracted from the firebox. I couldn't find Jack in the basement so I headed across the yard to the cafeteria. I saw him coming out the front door and ran to catch up. "Miss Barton wants you to come to our room, Jack."

"What she want?"

"Our radiators aren't working."

Without a word he hauled himself off toward the room, setting a rapid pace. I could hardly keep up with him. As we burst in, Miss Barton simply pointed. Jack went over, knelt beside the first radiator, loosened fittings, tightened fittings, banged with his wrenches, and finally the radiator spit and sputtered and steam began hissing. A minute later the second radiator, with connecting pipes, came to life and half the kids, who'd been whispering and talking, got up and crowded around the two radiators. As Jack left, Miss Barton allowed this for a while before she stood, draped her coat across the back of her chair, keeping her sweater on, and said, "All right, take your seats. We have work to do." She looked at me. "Thank you, Skeeter."

Pumped up, I finished the school day with a high level of confidence. But this was short-lived. On the way home my chain slipped again and the sudden drop of the pedal threw me forward toward the handlebars. I lost my balance and crashed down onto the sidewalk. Skinned up and humiliated before other kids walking along, I yanked my bike upright. "Damn! Damn!" I slammed it hard onto the concrete, which merely bent the fender down against the wheel. Angrily I grunted and tugged at the fender until I could get the wheel to turn. *Don't cut off your nose to spite your face.* I saw Malcolm Hughley walking ahead and pushed my bike fast to overtake him.

"What's the matter now, Skeeter?"

"Chain."

"I don't see why that'd be so hard to fix."

"You try, then."

When we reached his house on the corner we turned the bike upside down on the handlebars and seat and he went in to get some tools. As he undertook repairs I was glad for the chance to talk to him. As casually as I knew how I said, "Whatever it was I saw when I peeked through those old garage doors must be gone now. I don't think there is anything."

"What makes you say that?"

"It just looks like an old shack that needs tearing down."

He spoke in a husky voice, "That's the way they lull you, Skeeter. You see and hear nothing for a while then wham! They get you." He raised his head and looked at me through slitted eyes. "Don't let your guard down. There's something weird about the people who live there. And that spooky garage."

I gritted my teeth. "You know them?"

"Know them?" He bent back down. "I've heard about them. I've heard a lot."

He refused to say more. I watched impatiently as he fiddled with the chain, adjusted the sprocket, and went through all the adjustments I'd tried. Agitated and restless, I drifted over to the big magnolia in his side yard. All the kids climbed, but I had a particular talent for descending. I'd drop my feet into the air, hang by my hands, let go, and as I fell I'd grab the limb that I had been standing on. In this aerobatic feat I could be out of the tree and on the ground while the other boys inched their way down.

As Malcolm banged on my bicycle I climbed pretty high, then with a certain element of bravado commenced my descent. I dropped my feet from the limb I stood on, released my grasp on the one above and free-fell. For the first time ever, I missed. My right hand found purchase, my left slipped and I fell six feet to the hard ground beneath and hit flat on my back. The breath was knocked from me, my back and chest locked up, insentient, paralyzed. My eyes were wide open, staring up through the branches, frozen in a state of unbreathing shock.

In that instant of breathless mortality—ten seconds or less—I re-membered the evil presence just a few blocks away, and knew that I didn't want to be dead. Suddenly life in its worst forms was beautiful. Just moments ago I stood helpless, knowing all Malcolm's wrenching and tightening would not liberate me from disaster and fear. Now, paralyzed from the waist up, I felt warmth flooding my limbs. I spread out my fin-gers and touched the precious black earth. Objects above me released a cloud from my mind as though up out of a fog. With mouth open I tried to breathe but my lungs were anesthetized. All my senses—sight, smell, hearing—were unleashed as cosmic gases and my aliveness was more crystallized than when I could breathe. Malcolm had seen me fall and came away from the bike to stand over me. With the last ragged ribbon of breath I moaned, "Hit my back."

He pulled me up, opened his hand and struck me several sharp blows. My breath caught and I gulped saving air. In another few seconds I was on my feet. Malcolm had already turned away, oblivious of my revela-tion. A boy had fallen from a tree and knocked his breath out. That was all—nothing remarkable had occurred. He stood the bike up.

"Chain's stretched. You need to take it to somebody who can yank a link out."

"Yeah," I said with disgust. "I could've told you that."

I walked home with a strange surge of courage. There was a soreness up and down my spine, but I felt certain the bruises were temporary. My survival meant everything. I could scarcely grasp why losing my breath for a few seconds assured me that every breath I took had a reason.

* * *

A couple of days later Malcolm and I were playing marbles when I realized that he had contrived to do me out of my most prized boulders. Bigger, older, stronger, he was deadly with his shots. Generally I could hold my own, but by demonstrating a so-called new game of angles and rules he managed to weigh his strategy against me. Halfway through this game I stood and said sternly, "This isn't fair, Malcolm."

"What isn't fair?"

"The way you set this up. You know I don't have a chance."

"No? Then quit if you want to." He added under his breath, "Chicken."

Of course I couldn't quit and one by one I watched my boulders fall into his cache. Then something strange happened. His mother called him to come at once into the house and he ran off, leaving one of his bags of marbles among the oak roots near where we played. I saw that I now could retrieve some of my prized boulders, he probably would never notice. Besides, it would be no worse than what he'd done to me. But just as I was about to sneak over to his bag I remembered, *Two wrongs do not make a right*, the little proverb Miss Barton had drilled into us.

As I walked solemnly and thoughtfully away from temptation I tried to understand my own mind. I believed I was honest, intelligent, responsible, even creative. Even as I'd lain on my back with my breath knocked out it was as if I could feel my view of life being formed. I knew what was right and what was wrong. Still, the ups and downs, the unpredictable forces which I could never foresee and guard against, presented a frightening unknown to me.

11

Mat was dropping me off downtown. I was stuck in the back seat, hunkered down like a turtle hiding in its shell, trying to close my ears to the argument between Margaret and Mat.

"I *don't* understand why you're like this," she hissed. "This won't *hurt* you, Mat! You might actually *enjoy* it!"

"I'm not going."

"Well, I am! I *have* to." Characteristically emphasizing every few words, she spoke in bullets. "*Everybody* goes to the Valentine's dance."

"Go then."

Her stare became more defiant, she seemed to press herself away from him. "I'm *not* going alone."

This was a threat and I saw the flush of his cheeks, the ridge of veins in his neck. Margaret must have seen it, too, for she leaned toward him and crooned, "You know I could *never* go alone, Mat. And I don't want to go without you."

"Go with another girl. Go with your old man."

"Oh, you're so *stubborn!*" she cried. "How can you be so *thoughtless!*" Margaret sat silent for ten seconds before insisting, "I *have* to go, Mat. It's one of the nicest dances we have at the club. And I'm inviting you as politely as I know how."

"And I'm telling you no."

She sat back and gave up. "You're *hopeless!*"

How many fights they had like this that I didn't witness I could only imagine. Mat resented my presence, but such was the price of taking the car on days I had to be dropped off somewhere. They were both obstinate and self-centered, and Mat carried the additional burden of anger for the limitations imposed on him by his stature, by the lack of money and by a deeply ingrained defensiveness against lifetime bullying.

I felt pity for them both. Margaret could not imagine missing the elaborate Valentine's dance at the Country Club. She could get any date she wanted but knew how miserable they'd both be if she went with another boy. And while Mat ran around with several of the young men in her circle he held only disdain for these elaborate social affairs.

In this he was not alone. A couple of years back a young man named Ben Pruitt, enraged over his girlfriend's determination to present herself at one of the Cotillion dances, drew the club's big wrought iron entrance gates together and secured them with a heavy chain and padlock. Those who had already arrived, chaperones, orchestra, and servers, were wringing their hands because nobody was showing up for the dance, when they began to hear a great blasting of horns down on Cherokee Avenue. One of the boys went down, found the gates chained together and a congestion of impatient cars all up and down Cherokee. Traffic was snarled, a policeman had to be called to untangle the mess. Finally after another half hour a bolt cutter was appropriated, the chain cut and the gates open. The dance got underway an hour and a half late, half the evening spoiled. No one doubted the identity of the culprit, but nothing could be proved and besides, no one could find an ordinance against a jilted lover locking his girlfriend out of a dance. The ironic twist was that the girl was so impressed by the way Ben took matters in hand she gave herself willingly to him and they eventually married. I was pretty sure Mat would be capable of padlocking the Country Club's entrance gates, but this would imply that he cared more than he was willing to admit.

I was afraid this stand-off over the dance was but a flicker of a flame soon to explode. In this town, pedigree mattered. Even the love of my life, Judy Rollins, for whom I had drawn seven excruciatingly difficult horses, had dismissed me with poise. Most of us who grew up around Schaul Street thought little of pedigree, and really we pitied those who must distinguish themselves by hierarchy.

Margaret was devoted to Mat, and like our father he was so reticent in expressing emotion that when he did think himself in love it was explosive. The unwilling witness to so many fights between them, I felt certain that sooner or later he was going to get battered brutally. Their view of the world was simply too disparate.

Before I was let out of the car Margaret said tearfully, "I wish you wouldn't *be* this way, Mat. It makes it so hard for me to ... explain things."

"Don't explain, then. It's nobody's damn business."

"Oh, you just don't *know* how happy and how wretched you make me!"

This, I thought, was an accurate analysis. One thing I had to hand to Margaret — she was scaldingly honest.

* * *

One night Daddy was driving us home late from Grandmama's when we turned down Henry Avenue and passed the old garage. I was half asleep but awake enough to catch a glimmer of light through the sagging doors. A light! The haunted inside lit up! I wanted to cry out to Daddy to stop and look through the crack and tell me what he saw. But of course I said nothing, and remembering that I was barely awake began to wonder if I'd imagined it all.

Then a few days later I was pedaling past the looming two-story white house that sat beside the old garage when I was startled to discover three or four people on the wide front porch. The door was open, the screened door remained closed, and they seemed to be talking with someone behind the screen. I was surprised, having never been convinced the house was even occupied. But these were real people, who evidently had arrived in the shining black Lincoln parked at the curb. With the same sudden flair of courage I'd mustered when placing my two notes in the garage doors, I spun my bike and rode up the street, peering intently toward the house, the dark screen door and the strangers whom I felt could not possibly know what dangers their visit invited.

As I rode by, the screen door opened slightly and out came a slender arm passing something through. This appeared to be a large scroll or canvas of some sort. Strain as I might, I couldn't through the shadows of the porch discern more. Whatever the article was exchanged hands two or three times. I could detect some conversation but not faces or words. Just as I was about to turn the corner something happened which almost made me crash into the curb. The slender wrist which had passed the object through lifted and I had the startling impression that it was waving to me. What a shock! I felt as incriminated as a thief who has allowed his face to be seen. I had revealed my identity! I dug in and pedaled furiously, putting the unsuspecting victims behind.

* * *

Since Mat and I were now pretty savvy about what was going on, Daddy spoke more openly about his troubles with Mr. Montgomery and Chattahoochee Paint. One night at dinner he recounted in his usual quiet tone how he had been instructed to drive a load of paint out to one of the projects at Ft. Benning. He arrived at the job to find painters in white garb scurrying up and down extension ladders, scraping and priming windows and hauling drop cloths over their shoulders like burial shrouds. Daddy said he backed up his truck to a room assigned for storage, and a couple of painter's helpers came out to offload the truck.

As they transported paint cases into the storage room one of the Army inspectors arrived, a burly man with generous girth and suspicious eyes, wearing civilian clothes and an identification badge. He offered no conversation, merely walked up to Daddy and asked, "Monty send out a box for me?"

"I brought a load of paint."

"I hope that ain't all."

The inspector walked over to the truck and began to shuffle boxes around. In a few minutes he grunted and lifted out a box. "This comes to me," he said. "Personally."

Daddy saw that it was a case of Jack Daniels previously hidden by cases of paint. The man carried the booze to his truck, slipped it onto the floorboard and covered it with a rain slicker, making no effort to hide his actions. "I already paid Monty for this," he said. He then went into the building to make his so-called inspection. The workmen finished offloading and the job foreman came out to sign a receipt for the paint. As the boys began to load empty buckets onto the pickup Daddy asked, "What's this?"

"Mr. Montgomery makes us turn in all the empties." The foreman grinned slyly. "To be certain we don't sell his paint. Now, wonder why he'd think somebody might steal from him?"

When Daddy returned to the store Mr. Montgomery asked for the receipt for the cases. "I don't have one for every case." Daddy made no attempt to hide his disgust.

"You see what you're paid to see, Nathan. Keep your eyes closed and your mouth shut and you won't get into trouble."

Badly as Daddy needed this job he said sternly, "Don't ask me to go back out to any of those projects. I'm staying clear of them."

Daddy told us about this over the evening meal. His tone was solemn. "I'm surprised I didn't lose my job that minute."

"You didn't," said Mat, "because he's afraid if he fired you everything would come to light."

Mama's voice was just as grave as Daddy's. "They're just as guilty as he is. The only way that crooked man can get by with this is with the help of people who think nothing of cheating."

"I couldn't prove anything even if I wanted to."

"You think they could close the store?" Mat asked.

"Monty himself might close it if he can't use it as a front."

"What do you think you'd do?" I asked.

"I don't know." Daddy's expression was grave, but he wasn't beaten. "I still have the remodeling work, and maybe someday I'll have my own store. We'll manage. Remember, boys, everything you hear stays at this table."

I went into the living room, dropped down into the big upholstered chair and got busy on my lessons. Daddy changed clothes and hurried off to a night job, Mama cleaned up the kitchen and Mat took off with some boys. I slumped deeper into our frayed living room chair wondering why things like this happened. Daddy was honest to a fault, Mat and I worked wherever we could and treated everybody fairly. But it seemed that no matter how hard we tried things came up that we just couldn't prepare for.

12

I was afraid that if Margaret Howell didn't crush Mat he would do something else to get himself killed. Mat pretty much lived a life of his own. He ate, slept and practiced his trumpet at home, but his mind and spirit were elsewhere. It seemed to me he didn't much care what was going on at home. It was "out there" in the world somewhere that he would find his direction and his reckoning. His independence gave him strength, and his philosophy of life seemed to be skepticism. He was anti-sentimental and quick to hear false notes. He didn't much like school, he hated studying, was discontent and wanted a life unrestrained by age and circumstances. Worse, it seemed to me he either felt immortal or that he embraced a kind of death wish, rejecting sanity as a governing factor in his life. Of course it was always possible that since Mat kept his inner self to himself, as Daddy and most of the Harding's did, my perceptions might not have been accurate.

The next crazy thing Mat did began when we went to the stock car races. My father could seldom afford money for movies or holidays, but occasionally he managed to get hold of tickets to the races. He, Mat, Mat's friend Pudge Brewster, and I piled into our car and crossed the Chattahoochee River into Alabama, following a string of cars out to the track. We parked in a grass field, got out and joined spectators streaming toward the gates and bleachers.

"I'm freezing my ass off," grumbled Pudge.

"You should have worn more clothes," I said. He had not planned to be out and had brought only a light windbreaker.

"Brilliant suggestion, Skeeter."

"We used to keep an old Army blanket in the trunk," Mat said, "but I took it out last time I cleaned the car."

"What was that for?" Pudge grinned. "To throw around your girl when she got cold?"

We got our tickets and filed through the gates. People all around were wrapped in blankets and heavy coats. Down on the infield cars were warming up, the roar of unmuffled engines reverberating like disorganized drum rolls.

"See that number twenty-seven?" said Pudge. "He'll grab the lead right away. He's in the first race."

"How do you know?"

"He's a devil on wheels."

"I like the car with the dragon painted down the side," I said. "It's spitting fire."

"Yeah, but he's got that car so dolled up he'll be scared of caving in something."

"These cars bang each other all the time," Mat said. "They roll 'em, too."

"Somebody might wreck?" I was incredulous.

"Every spectator here's hoping to see a big crash," said Pudge.

All around us men were making bets on the races. "Five dollars on number three in the second."

"I'll match that. It's like taking candy from a baby."

"Where's Armstrong?"

"In the first."

"Yeah, who'll give me ten Armstrong won't take it?"

Pudge said, "Armstrong's number twenty-seven. I told you."

A tall blond woman laughed, "I'll hold the money."

"I have a dollar," I said. "Should I bet on something?"

"Keep your money, Skeeter," said Daddy. "It never pays to gamble."

Prior to the races a ramp was towed out onto the track. A red Ford sedan came roaring down, swept up the ramp on two wheels, and tilted crazily to one side. It ran about a hundred feet before finally crashing back down to scream around the turn.

"He nearly turned over!" I exclaimed.

"He knows exactly the speed he needs to get up on two wheels," Mat said. "Too much or too little and he goes over."

A second ramp was towed out and a sleek Studebaker squealed down the track, went airborne and crashed down the descending ramp with a great clamoring of springs and body.

"You see that, Skeeter?" said Pudge. "Think you'd like to fly a car?"

"Oh, sure. You bet."

The races began with souped-up stock cars — Fords, Chevys, Pontiacs, Cadillacs — and Mat and Pudge bet between themselves just for fun.

We stayed through the last race. Then as we worked our way down from the bleachers, Pudge asked, "You ever go out to the drag strip, Mat?"

Mat gave him a hard look and shook his head as if to say, "Keep quiet."

Evidently this wasn't conversation for Daddy's ears.

Out loud Pudge said, "That was some pretty good racing."

"I liked the jumps best," I said.

I caught a look in his eye and suspected that he and Mat had already contrived something outlandish. Within a week, I found out that the two boys, enlisting the help of some of their cronies, were foraging county woods to find a washed-out pulpwood road split by a creek with steep banks. When they discovered just the right place they appropriated bush axes to clear the limbs, dead wood and debris from either side of the stream. Pudge would use his own little Ford coupe and they would flip a coin to see who would drive.

One of the boys warned, "I don't think you'll make it. The gap's too wide."

"Naw. I'll clear easily," said Pudge.

"Besides, the angle's wrong. The landing side's too high."

I heard enough to follow the proceedings and appealed to Mat not to do it. "I'm afraid something bad could happen."

"Forget it. We're all set."

"But you won't drive!"

"Depends on how the coin falls."

"Then let me go," I pleaded.

"Nothing doing. You keep quiet."

I knew this meant I'd be kept in the dark. "Please don't try it, Mat. You could get killed. And Pudge is your friend. You don't want to see him die, do you?"

"There can be worse things."

How many risks would my brother take, how many times would he cut himself off from the outside world before he paid an awful toll? Perhaps it was the same with all his high school friends. *Birds of a feather flock together.*

When everything was ready, they chose a clear Saturday afternoon and several cars caravanned out to the secret country road, a mixed bag of boys and girls who knew Mat and Pudge or had just heard about the big event. A coin was flipped, and Pudge was the driver. He tapped Mat on the shoulder. "Maybe on the second run," he said, "if there is a second run."

Pudge then made a display of prancing around, checking wheels and tightening his belt. When he had played this bravado to the hilt, he climbed in and buckled on a football helmet.

"Anybody wanna ride?"

They all declined.

Mat leaned into the window. "Hold her steady. You don't want to hit the launch pad at an angle."

"Gotcha. Let's see what this baby'll do."

Pudge revved up the engine and gunned it. The tires bit in and he came tearing down the old sawmill road, flew off the near bank, went airborne for perhaps two seconds and crashed belly first into the clay bank on the other side. When the car slammed down it broke both axles, twisted the drive shaft and snapped his neck forward so hard the only reason his ribs weren't broken was because he'd had the good sense to place a small pillow between his chest and the steering wheel. By the time the spectators jumped the creek and ran to him he had dragged himself from the car, groaning, both hands on his neck. Half-dazed, he muttered, "Next time I'll make it."

They got him into one of the other cars and raced him to the emergency room. No bones had been shattered but the suffering he endured in his neck for the next few weeks was punishment enough. Plus, he was without a car. He took fury from his father and it was a couple of months before he was allowed to drive any car again.

"If Pudge had handed you the keys would you have tried that stupid thing?" I asked Mat.

"Maybe. I wouldn't want to have to buy him another car."

"What if he'd broken his neck. Or his back. It could've been you."

"Yeah. Could've been."

I was terrified of the things Mat might get himself into. But I saw that he was making things happen, while I only waited for something momentous to occur.

* * *

With Pudge grounded, Mat and their other friends pitched in to provide transportation. This threw Pudge and me together occasionally. He would sit in the front seat, me in the back, waiting for Mat to finish band practice or some after school requirement, and he would fill me in on various events. He still wore his neck brace which looked horrible with ink smears and lipstick smears, and when he turned to watch my reactions he had to shift his torso and slide forward on the seat, grinning mischievously. He told me about a big fight between Mat and Margaret.

Mat was bringing Margaret home from a date, and when they pulled into her driveway she burst into tears. "My parents are making me *go away* this summer!"

Stunned, Mat said, "Go where?"

"To Arizona, of all places. We have relatives there."

"Why!"

"Why do you think? They say we're seeing too much of each other."

"What do *you* think?"

"You *know* what I think!" she insisted.

"You can damn sure tell me if you want to break it off."

"Mat, don't be angry with *me*! This is *their* idea."

"And what do you tell them?"

"That I'm not going…I don't *want* to go."

"But they're making you."

"Yes. They're making me."

"Bullshit."

"What do you mean bullshit?"

"They can't make you do anything."

"You're mistaken about *that*, Mat. It could be a threat, but I know they mean it."

"So." He spoke through clenched teeth, "It's either drop me or send you off for the summer."

She sniffed louder as all his flesh went tense. Mat hardly knew her parents, but he knew the town's social theocracy and didn't give a damn what they found lacking in him.

"Tell them you're not going, Margaret. You can twist them around your finger."

"Not when it comes to something like this. They go *crazy* over their stupid ideas. I've heard it all my life. So-and-so should marry this sort of man, so-and-so is that one's kind of girl. It's a clan system."

"Screw the clan," he said.

"That's what I'm *doing*, don't you see? With you."

"I see you're going to have to make a decision."

"I've made a decision. I want to stay with you."

Much as he hated this sort of snobbery Mat probably was jealous that he was excluded from it. He insisted she could do what she wanted, she protested that absolute defiance was impossible. She could scream and cry, but they *were* her parents and she lost control when they put their foot down.

"We'll just take off and see what they say about that," he said bitterly.

"Take off! Are you *insane*? Take off where?"

"Hit the road. Let them try and find us."

"You wouldn't *dare* and you know it. Nor would I. You're saying this just to see if I'd do it!" She scrubbed her eyes and turned her pretty, pouting mouth to him. "What am I supposed to *do*, Mat? My parents insist I'm spending too much time with you. You're mad because you think I can defy them. But I *can't*. I have to finish school, I have to go to college. Oh, why can't they just leave me *alone* and let me be happy!"

"Happy?" His tone was biting. "Is that something you deserve for being born with a silver spoon?"

"Oh, you can be so *mean*!" She broke into tears again. "I don't *want* to be miserable all the time!"

"It's all about money isn't it? Tell them I said go to hell."

"Oh, *that* would make them respect you, wouldn't it?"

Mat was in pain but too furiously independent to relinquish the point. "It's up to you, Margaret. Go ahead and let them stamp your life."

"Now what does *that* mean?"

"You know what it means. If you choose to be just like them we don't have a lot in common!"

When Pudge told me about this fight I felt sorry for Mat. I had no hope that he would tell me anything, but I searched his face to see if he was miserable. His expression was hard and inscrutable. He could hide behind his anger, his toughness, but I was afraid he might do something crazy. He might convince Margaret to run away with him, never to be heard of again—not so much because he was deliriously in love but to show them he could.

* * *

Whether Mat's anger over Margaret and life in general precipitated another near disaster—again, he could have gotten himself beaten to a pulp—I didn't know. I only knew that watching him sometimes was like watching one of those war movies in which some devil-may-care infantryman fended off an overwhelming number of attackers knowing that sooner or later he would be killed. Nor did I know why this one boy, whose name was Dennis Vallarta, was gunning for Mat. Evidently, they'd had words and Dennis was out to settle a grudge.

It occurred in our own driveway. The first thing Mama and I knew was when we heard Mat outside our kitchen window snarling and swearing. I ran to the window and looked out. Dennis and about four of his cronies were halfway up our driveway, Mat standing twenty feet away in front of our garage. I heard him say, "Get your ass off my property!" and with fear in my heart I saw the blood-red infusion of rage that distorted his fine features.

Mat was not the sort who looked for trouble. Except for some particular girl—at this time Margaret Howell—he hardly cared enough for anybody to allow them to touch him in any way. But when a fight was inevitable his fists were cutting and swift, and his unsuspecting opponents seldom landed a solid blow. He ducked under, bobbed, feigned, with an almost uncanny sense of where the next swing would come from, and his ability to anticipate a movement confused and intimidated his enemy. His contemptuous rebellion invited outweighed, outclassed threats, but even when he hit the ground, dazed, sometimes scarcely conscious, he came up swinging.

I heard Mama start out the back door and ran to catch her. Mat had a Coca-Cola bottle in his hand. He must have seen the others coming and grabbed the bottle off the back porch. As soon as the boys saw Mama there was a renewed ripple of tension, but they did not withdraw.

"What's going on here?" she demanded.

136

"Nothing." Mat spoke with a face of stonelike anger.

She turned to the boys. "What business do you have here?"

"We're talkin' to Mat."

She moved forward. I reached to tug at her skirt but my hand fell short. There was something about her I'd never witnessed before. She was such a quiet, shy woman I was surprised to see the tension in her motions and hear the raw challenge in her voice. One of the boys mumbled something under his breath which prompted a snicker. I could see Mat growing more furious.

Dennis Vallarta was a lumbering, husky boy with big hands and grimy nails. He worked in his father's automobile repair shop and could, I had little doubt, put Mat down with his strong arms and brute fists. He turned his head to say something to the boys and they snickered again.

Mama moved two more steps toward them. "Get out of my yard or I'll call the police."

To my surprise they backed off. With another incoherent epithet they turned and drifted down the driveway. I exhaled a deep breath, thinking it was over. But I misjudged Mat. His pent-up rage had to find vent, his very skin burned revenge. Without taking a step he drew his arm back and threw the Coke bottle at Dennis's retreating head. How his aim could have been so deadly accurate I'll never know. The bottle struck Dennis on the left side of his skull with a perceptible *whang!* and crashed into the foundation of the house next door. Dennis gave a shocked, painful cry, staggered forward and almost went down. My blood rushing with sheer panic, I expected the whole bunch to turn on Mat, maybe Mama and me, too. To my amazement none of them spun around even to look back. The other boys had seen and heard the bottle crack off Dennis's head, saw him fall forward, but not one of them so much as interrupted his retreat. It was unbelievable. I could never have explained it. They disappeared down the street, Dennis holding a handkerchief to his head.

Mama looked at Mat with cold gravity but I was further amazed that she uttered not a word. I think maybe she was sad for him, enraged at him, and wished she could protect him and all us children from our own defenseless fears and confusions. Mat spun on his heels and resumed cleaning up our old Chevy as if no near fatal catastrophe had occurred. I wondered why Dennis hadn't retaliated. With his backup he could have stomped Mat. I wondered if in that split second his dull brain realized the arm that drove him almost to his knees was more powerful than skinny Mat—some invisible fury which could have overwhelmed him.

* * *

I was walking to school with Malcolm, Jean Gresham and John Shoulder (John had long since had all the stitches out of his leg but still walked with a slight limp, either from habit or to get a little more mileage out of his knife wound), when I noticed an extension ladder standing against the house across the street from the old garage. Mrs. Grossman was having her cornices painted. It gave me an idea. When I returned home after school I dug out the cheap binoculars I'd received a couple of Christmases earlier and took them along as I pedaled back toward Wynnton for my papers. Mrs. Grossman was old and if she happened to look out the window and see me she'd think little of it. I parked my bike, ran across her yard and scurried up the ladder for a bird's eye view of the haunted old garage. High up, I trained my binoculars and everything was brought closer to me.

Though I chewed my lip with excitement my first impression was one of disappointment. I saw a single door on the side, with the grassless, path-worn dirt leading to it. The siding had deteriorated beyond hope of scraping and painting. The roof had been repaired so many times with metal, shingles and roll roofing it was a patchwork of faded colors and shapes, and the outlookers were rotting away. On the far side of the yard was a low, half-collapsed brick wall, and the cat I'd seen lounging on the fence sat majestically on this wall, bathing itself. The screened rear porch of the house was forbidding and dark, and though I searched for a hint of light through one of the windows I discovered none. The sheer ordinariness of the garage, the house and the yard was so anti-climactic I wished for some frightening revelation. Only my imagination could create from this dull and damp-looking habitat anything threatening, yet it suddenly dawned on me that such was exactly the sort of disguise malevolent spirits maintained. I retreated down the ladder confused and half-certain that the vile thing which occupied this stinking old garage represented all the frightening things in my little world. As I bagged my papers and rode furiously around my route, I thought of the notes I'd written and received through the crack in the twisted doors and felt my blood run cold. I yearned for someone to confide in.

Then I began to wonder if the ghost of the garage acted alone. Much as I wanted to put this devil behind I was hooked in a kind of horrified fascination, as if I were in a jungle being stalked by a killer animal and the only hope for escape was not to let my watchfulness stray for an instant. It seemed my only weapon of defense was *closer* vigilance, and that night I sat at our dining room table and with trembling hand wrote my third note. At first it was going to be, "I dare you to show your face," but finally in a kind of conciliatory appeal I decided on, "Do you have a friend?"

Awaiting the same agonizing scene as before—a sunny afternoon, cars going by, people on the street—I ran up to the dilapidated doors, jammed my paper into the crack and hurried away.

Within a day or two the note had disappeared, but after a week, finding no response, I decided perhaps it was over at last. Then one afternoon I glimpsed protruding from the crack a fragment of gray-white paper. So it was not over at all. But I couldn't bring myself to let go—the wound aching for the knife. I ran to the door, grabbed the paper and fled. When finally I forced myself to unfold the note I read my own words, "Do you have a friend?" then down beneath, in the same patient calligraphy, "My work. And darkness."

A cold lump fell in my stomach. A friend of darkness! The concealment of shadows! The cloak of wickedness!

But what unsettled me most was a perfectly hand-drawn sketch on the lower half of the page. It was of a bicycle and a boy riding it. Across the handlebars was a *Ledger* canvas carrier bag, and the rider, bent slightly to pump, was looking to one side, with an expression of anxiety. For a long moment I could only stare. Finally there was no further doubt. The boy on the bicycle was me.

13

I'd left the house on my bike and started up Schaul when I heard loud voices bursting from the Gresham house. It sounded like a bitter fight. Jean's cries of outrage crashed through the screened porch, while her mother swore and railed in senseless defense. The grandmother's shrill words punctuated the exchange like missiles. All the neighbors had overheard such battles, which never seemed to resolve anything.

With a final defiant cry Jean suddenly ran out into her front yard. Seeing me, she spun away as if ashamed, and ran down the driveway toward her backyard. She threw herself head on against the closed doors of the small garage, pressed her face into her raised arm and with her clenched fist pounded over and over on the door. I was startled by this violence and torn with pity and confusion. Something twisted and turned in my breast, I felt Jean's anguish, I hated her mother for causing it, and wondered how the parent of a sweet daughter could be so self-centered as to abandon her precious gift to emotional destruction. It reminded me again how many ways a child can love her mother.

I wheeled away and hastened on. Then something stopped me. I knew I had little physical courage, but a courage seemed to rise from within, to tell me what to do. I turned, rode down the Gresham driveway and jumped off my bike. Jean kept her face buried in her arms as she wept. As her fist hammered again and again on the splintered door I ran over, caught her arm and forced it down to her side. Her arm was stiff as iron, her chest rose and fell with deep sobs and all I knew to do was stand quietly, grasping her hand. Finally she turned from the wall and sank down into a patch of grass.

"Jean," I said, "I'm sorry."

She buried her head in her arms.

"Why does she do this?" I asked.

She huddled down, trembling and weeping. "I don't know."

"Can't you get her some help?"

"She doesn't want help."

I could hardly comprehend this—how any temporary escape could be worth the hell that followed. Why anybody would ever start with something like this, knowing how it could destroy their brains and their lives was beyond my grasp.

I searched for something that would make Jean feel better. "Want to go riding?"

"My bike's broken."

"We can ride double."

"Don't you have to throw papers?"

"It can wait."

"No, Skeeter, I have to stay here."

I hated to leave her, yet wanted to get away from this place where something vile seemed to poison the air. "Okay," I said. "I hope you won't beat on the garage anymore."

She took a deep breath. "No, I won't."

"I know she doesn't mean to hurt you, Jean. I guess she can't help herself."

She looked up, removed her glasses to dry her tears and gazed at me with sad eyes. "Do you know sometimes she doesn't even have money for my lunch? If it weren't for my grandmamma...Oh, Skeeter, let's not ever do anything like this."

"We won't."

"Not even smoke. Promise me you won't smoke!"

Every man I knew smoked, even boys Mat's and Pudge's age smoked, but I said, "Okay, I won't. Besides, I tried it once and didn't like it."

"Don't try again. Please! Sometimes just once and…you're done for!"

As I rode away I felt terrible for poor Jean. We had our share of troubles, but I could hardly imagine what it would be like to lose my mother.

* * *

As I rode down Henry Avenue I was startled to see our Sunday School teacher Mr. Preston in the yard of the big looming house in front of the evil garage. There were two or three other men with him, looking around and making some sort of inspection. I realized Mr. Preston's real estate business took him all over town, but to witness a man I knew, alive, vibrant, smoking his cigar, walking jauntily around this gloomy place sent a thrill of danger through me.

On Sunday I mustered courage to ask him about it. "That old house over on Henry. Does someone really live there?"

He seemed surprised that I should ask. "Of course. It's a well-built structure. Two solid floors. Could use some fixing up, though."

"Who are they?"

"The Zimmermans. Nice people."

"How many?"

"Three, I think. The parents and a grown son."

Almost accusingly, I said, "They keep all their blinds down. You never see anybody! And that old garage —"

"Well, things are strange around there." Mr. Preston, a man of mischief himself, apparently caught something of my anxiety. He pulled the cigar from his mouth and squinted at me. "You can't judge a book by its cover, Skeeter."

So Mr. Preston knew some proverbs, too. But it did nothing to allay my apprehension. If I told him about my notes, about the sketch of the boy on a bicycle, he'd just think me meddling.

And I doubted that he could clarify for me much about church, either. I hadn't totally recovered from the betrayal by Mr. Gerber. I wanted to live, to do something daring, to save a life, to see something beautiful. But things confused me. In our congregation was a young woman who'd been widowed by the war, a single mother with two children who struggled to hold her little family together. She always brought her children to church and always had a cheerful smile. Then there was Mrs. Arlington who was loaded to the hilt, the wife of a prominent stockbroker, who was so miserable she took her own life by drinking two cans of liquid Drano, a horrible, excruciating death. I wondered why she did this. We heard that she moaned and screamed. Did she believe she had to suffer, that physical pain would dull emotional pain? I wondered how two women who attended the same church could look at circumstance through such different lenses.

Then there was little Kathy Fiscus, a child who fell into an abandoned well out West. For three days I stayed glued to the news as rescue workers drilled and dug trying to reach her. I imagined poor Kathy lodged into the shaft, terrified, crying, cold, thirsty, pleading for her mommy. It made me sick with pity and fear. I wanted so much for her to be rescued, I wanted her to see glorious sunshine again, to live a happy and resurrected life. For three days she hung on, but when the rescue team finally reached her she was dead. I felt wrenched inside. I knew I would never forget little Kathy Fiscus who lived far off yet whose death struck me in a peculiar way—a spiritual way, as though there were some sort of invisible vein connecting us. I wondered if her family believed she was dead and gone forever, or that they would someday see her again. I wished I knew.

And Mat didn't help either. At sixteen, he viewed religion with doubt and contempt. I tried to sweet talk him into believing while he taunted me for dressing up to "play church." Of course he thought he knew more than I'd ever know, but in some ways I believed I was smarter than he. I delivered my papers every day, even in the most horrid weather, stuffed my few dollars into the cigar box, paid my *Ledger* bill on Saturday or

Monday, and stayed busy, which I suppose was a good thing. As Miss Barton frequently cautioned us, *An idle mind is the devil's workshop.*

* * *

Mother said, "Aunt Harrell wants you to spend the night with her Friday, Skeeter."

My heart sank. I knew sooner or later it would be my turn again, and though it was a chance to earn a dollar there were few things I dreaded more. "Do I have to?"

"You know it isn't right to leave Aunt Harrell alone. All you have to do is sleep."

Sleep. If it were only that simple. I was terrified of her old two-story house with its creaking stairs and groaning walls.

Aunt Harrell was a distant aunt through some complex interrelations of marriage, well-off but extremely stingy. She had a live-in housekeeper who had to be given an occasional night off to go home to her own family, and one of us nephews was required to come over, sleep in a big extra bedroom, eat a sparse breakfast, collect our dollar, and vanish.

Despite my anxiety, on Friday I rode up to her roomy white house just before dark, knocked, and stood listening to her padded footfalls. Aunt Harrell threw the bolt, let me in and offered me milk and cookies. She sat with me at her breakfast room table as I ate these heartily. "How is school, Skeeter? Are you making good grades?"

"I guess so."

"Would you believe I went to Wynnton when I was a little girl?"

"You must have lived in this house a long time."

"A long time, yes. Don't forget to wash behind your ears."

Aunt Harrell always reminded us to wash behind our ears.

We had a dutiful conversation, but it was evident that she paid little attention to what I contributed and after this brief dialogue said, "Well, you know where your room is. We'll see each other in the morning," whereupon she retired to her bedroom, locked the door, and from my perspective was no longer relevant.

This was about the time I began to hate myself—because I feared the dark, the unknown, the future, my own imagination. The big rooms with their high ceilings, tall windows and heavy draperies, two ornate staircases, solid paneled doors, and thick carpets which smelled of musk and lemon, the air as motionless and insentient as a vault—all encapsulated my indefinable fears much as the old garage on Henry did. My only hope was to undress, jump into bed, cover up and hide myself in the merciful abandon of sleep. I took off my clothes and draped them over a chair, but left my socks on.

As always, sleep eluded me. With lights out I began to hear every imaginable moan, groan, creak, whisper, grunt and thump and rustle that an old structure can make, like the straining of an ancient ship. The room itself, emitting the faint scent of age and air freshener, came alive with such sinister noises that I stared into blackness expecting at any moment for ghostly hands to close on my throat. I had no doubt that the evil forces of the old garage on Henry could track me at will, and that the danger was not merely of a physical nature, but, perhaps more threatening, of my wild imagination. Lying rigid as a board, I told myself that darkness brought no menacing changes in walls chalky with age, that my fear was merely irrational and self-destructive, but none of these inner persuasions provided relief.

As I lay faint-hearted I wondered if anyone—my mother, my father, brother—anyone understood how pitiful fear is to the fearful. Something vise-like and crushing gripped my chest, I could hardly breathe. The blood rioted in my arms and I could actually feel the rapid beating of my heart. I felt that at any moment I could die and hoped it would come quickly, without pain. But I knew I wouldn't die. I would slowly suffocate, revive, suffocate, and on top of this was the self-loathing I felt for allowing fear to overcome me.

After an hour's trembling struggle I slipped out of bed, dressed and crept downstairs, hoping the bumps and creaks of the stairway wouldn't wake Aunt Harrell. I didn't know what she would do. Come out of her room screaming; or perhaps she had the fortitude to carry a shotgun and would blow me away. A sparse distribution of night lights illuminated the creepy walls and at the end of the hall I found the one phone with which Aunt Harrell indulged herself. I called our number and after a few rings my mother answered sleepily. "Mama," I whispered, "I'm scared."

"What? What?" She was trying to wake up.

I held back the tears. "Can I come home?"

There was a moment of rebuke and arguing—I couldn't possibly leave Aunt Harrell, I had to stop thinking of myself. But as the urgency and helpless terror in my voice deepened she finally sighed, "I'll try to wake Mat. We can't leave Aunt Harrell alone."

Fifteen minutes later my brother, angry, grim, disgusted, tapped on the downstairs front door. I slipped the latch and let him in. He spat one bitter accusation, "Baby!" then proceeded upstairs where within minutes I had no doubt he'd be asleep in the bed I left.

I grabbed my jacket, ran out into the cold, jumped on my bike, and rode furiously through black streets glowing eerily under the arc of occasional street lights, detouring blocks out of the way to avoid Henry Avenue, and turned onto Schaul in minutes that seemed like hours. After making sure I arrived home, Mama went back to bed and I fell into my own bed where security waited like an old friend.

I slept fitfully, angry at myself, embarrassed, thinking how much harder it was, or should have been, for me to forge around my paper route than to sleep under Aunt Harrell's thick feather quilts.

Morning light brought renewed peace, but hang-dogged and wary, I tried to get out of the house before Mat came home. He returned early and the first thing he did was wave a crisp one dollar bill under my nose. "Easiest dollar I ever made."

I ground my teeth, coveting the dollar, and as I rode down Wildwood I looked over at Aunt Harrell's and saw that it looked no more spooky than any other old house with its narrow portico and ranked white columns and side yard swing.

* * *

I had just thrown a paper at a house way up a hill off Sixteenth Street and had taken a short cut to Carter Avenue when I was attacked by a pack of dogs. I saw them coming, five or six of various breeds and sizes running wild and frenetic. They charged me with shrieking barks and growls, thin lips stretched back on bared teeth. Terrified, I jumped off my bike, trying to station it between them and me. "Stop! Stop!" They circled to my side, snapping at my ankles and calves. I jumped back over again, holding the bike between us. They split up to attack me from both sides. Sharp teeth tore through my socks, puncturing flesh.

Tears stinging my eyes, I kicked and yelled, but not until a man ran out from a yard swinging a rake did the pack break off and run on up the street, leaving me trembling with pain.

"You okay, son? They bite you?"

"Yes, sir, a few times." I dabbed at my tears, feeling the warm wetness of blood trickling down my calves.

"Damn dogs. They ought to be shot."

That's what I wanted to do—corner them and pick them off one by one. I swung onto my bike and peddled hard, continuing to deliver papers. When I finally finished and rode heavily into our driveway I felt as if I carried weights and chains. At least my old Schwinn hadn't let me down this time. But for using it as a shield the bites could have been worse.

As I walked in, Mama asked, "What's the matter?"

I pulled up my pant leg. "Dogs."

She bent to look, then went to fetch peroxide and iodine. "Where'd this happen?"

"Over on Carter."

"You recognize the dogs?"

I shook my head.

When Daddy came home she had me show him the punctures. "He could get rabies," she said.

"Mad dogs don't usually act like that."

"Maybe you should go see."

I knew the last thing Daddy wanted was to go out again, and I didn't want to go either. It was nearly dark when we drove over to Carter. We saw some dogs but I couldn't say I recognized any of them. We returned home silently, and Mama shook her head. "Maybe he'd better have rabies shots."

My fear was renewed. "I don't want them!" I'd heard about rabies shots. They were painful and expensive.

I could tell that Daddy was weighing the cost. Finally, he said, "We'll keep an eye on him."

"If he gets lockjaw it'll be too late."

My stomach churned. Lockjaw. I might never speak again! I might have to be fed through a straw stuck between my teeth. I might die! Without hearing a word, I knew what Mama and Daddy were thinking. That money was so tight they couldn't afford urgent medical treatment for their children.

I slipped into my room and sat on the bed. Through the window the stars glittered blue and silver. Wispy ribbons of milk white were drawn across the sky like the veil of a bride. I shivered, wondering if I would have to throw papers forever, if I would always be afraid. When other boys were taking off their shirts to feel the sun and girls were drawing hopscotch squares on the streets, would I always struggle to get fillings for my teeth or unfrayed underwear? Still, I felt power in my independence. And I believed I could do anything. This thought reassured me. I could take care of myself, I could rise to the demands made on me no matter what—but I was afraid of the dark. It was confusing.

I reached down to tenderly touch the bites on my ankles and calves, smeared red with iodine now like Indian war paint. Tiny flecks of dried blood traced the tooth marks. The punctures were superficial, sliced at a glancing blow, but enough to carry a deadly disease. I wondered what would happen to my family if I contracted rabies.

Don't cross a bridge before you come to it.

I tried to put the day behind, but for the next couple of weeks I noticed Mama and Daddy watching me warily. I didn't know what they were looking for. Maybe I'd start foaming at the mouth. Maybe I'd begin talking through my teeth like a man with his jaw wired shut. Nothing happened. Eventually our fears abated. But for a long time, the sight of two or three dogs running together horrified me. I was a capable young businessman and this fact meant something to me. But I saw that self-reliance, valuable as it was, was never going to be easy.

14

I ran from the bed to the living room hearth to pull on my clothes. The floor was cold, the walls were cold, the rooms were cold. Half an hour earlier Daddy had lit the small space heater in the living room and I stood as close to it as possible to dress. My toes curled from the icy brick hearth and I yearned for summer. No call from Mama or an alarm clock was needed to wake me. Outside our bedroom window was a mimosa tree into which blue jays flung themselves every morning, screeching and brawling. If I tried to sneak around the corner of the house with my B-B gun or slingshot the jays were gone in a flash.

As I dressed sleepily I heard snatches of conversation between Mama and Daddy in the kitchen. "Sooner or later a crook gets caught," she said.

"My guess is Monty can buy himself out of most anything."

Despite the threat of unemployment, it seemed to me Daddy didn't let his spirits down, or he was just good at hiding his feelings. I once saw him almost throw up at a football game because a fight broke out in the bleachers below and he thought it involved Mat. Until then I had never suspected Mat's brawls bothered him very much.

As Daddy started to leave for work he said, "I'll need to eat as soon as I get home tonight. We're starting a new job and want to get a few things done before dark."

"Where's the job?" Mama asked.

"Just around the block. Over on Henry."

This snagged my attention. "Where on Henry?"

"The corner," he said. "Henry and Francis."

"Not the big white house with the old garage that comes up to the sidewalk."

"That's the one. We've got to jack up the porch and repair exterior trim."

"You can't work on that house!" I cried.

He had his hand on the doorknob. "Why not?"

"It's dangerous!"

"Dangerous?" He shook his head. "I wouldn't say so. Just some cornice work and underpinning."

"No, I mean … I mean the garage —"

But he was gone — to what destiny I could only dread.

I remembered our Sunday School teacher Mr. Preston saying the old house needed work, but I could never have imagined that Daddy and my Uncle Talbot would contract to do it. They could not know the dangers that lurked there. At school I found it just about impossible to concentrate. Outside the windows, the ground was frostbitten and on Wynnton Road the plate glass fronts of King's Grocery ran drips like tears. Everything seemed thrown into a shocking light — mortality was identified by a power pole guide wire, a telephone call box, cars swishing through wet gutters. Miss Barton scolded a girl for her poor script. "You can do better than this, Imogene, if you try." It felt like barbs in my flesh.

As if these weren't biting spears of clarity, Mr. Buxton came into the classroom to substitute for Miss Barton for an hour. The air grew tense, an invisible fog of tension freezing every pupil at his desk, but with his beak nose and sharp mind Mr. Buxton plowed through the currents like the prow of a ship. "Sit up straight and put your feet on the floor." Had we not obeyed, the lesson would have been rigid, but since we complied obediently he took out a book and read to us from Poe's *The Raven*, which he loved. It seemed to me that Mr. Buxton had a hawk's vision, a surgeon's stoutheartedness, but I realized my impressions might be totally different from another student's. Finally he left the classroom, school was over, and he hurried down the halls ringing the bell like someone disgruntled, comical, and possessed.

Books under my arms, I hurried home. As I passed the old garage I said out loud, "You better not hurt him!" All I could think of was Daddy and Uncle Talbot exposing themselves to this yard and garage!

At home I grabbed my usual peanut butter and banana sandwich, then hurried back to our pickup station and dogged my old Schwinn around my paper route. I knew that about now Daddy and Uncle Talbot would be getting to work on the white house, and prayed my bike wouldn't let me down. I rode so fast and threw the papers so furiously a couple of them tore across the front page. Ordinarily I would slam on brakes, turn back and drop another paper, but today I couldn't bring myself to stop. When I finally slid the last edition down the last walkway on Thirteenth Street it was nearly dark and without taking a break or slowing my speed I headed straight back toward Henry and Francis. Daddy and Uncle Talbot had finished for the day and were gathering up their tools. I was relieved to find them alive and intact. By the darkened pyramidal shadows under the wood porch I saw that they had managed to snake the big house jacks in place and level up the sagging joists under the wide front porch.

"Hi, man," said Daddy.

Uncle Talbot broke off to shake hands. "Good to see you, Skeeter."

"Can I help?"

"We're about to pull out." Daddy looked at my bike. "We need to get you a light. You shouldn't be riding after dark."

I straddled the bar, putting both feet down. "Did anything happen?"

"Anything like what?"

"Do you know the people in that house?"

"Your uncle knows them."

"You aren't going to do anything to the old garage, are you?"

"That old shack out back? Where the bodies are?"

Hot pricks ran across my scalp. I thought Daddy would long since have forgotten my report last summer of peeking through the cracks in the sagging doors. Even in near darkness I could discern an impish smile cross his lips, much like the smile Mr. Preston had given me when I questioned him about the house. "Naw. Better stay away from back there."

I realized Daddy was needling me, but I knew it was because he couldn't conceive of anybody living in the decaying garage.

"How long will you be working here?"

"Oh, off and on for a while. Probably won't do the painting until spring."

My heart sank. I thought they'd be finished in a few days. I climbed onto my bike and pedaled thoughtfully home, passing five yards from the old garage. I held my speed, resisting the impulse to dig in. Daddy and Uncle Talbot hadn't pulled off, but it wasn't their presence that provided me an extra shot of boldness. When I looked over at the dilapidated doors they looked simply black, silent, and isolated. I was struck neither with feelings of fear nor of harm. For the first time this solitary dwelling just looked lonely. Ramshackle as it was I knew that sooner or later the old monstrosity would have to be torn down. In the semi-dark stillness it looked lonely, and I felt strangely sympathetic.

* * *

One weekend Pudge and his girlfriend Amy double-dated with Mat and Margaret, and after the movie Margaret said, "Let's do something crazy."

"Like what?" said Mat.

"Mmm. Let's go climb the water tower."

"That *is* crazy. Especially for a girl."

The old abandoned water tower was located out near the post, on top of a high hill. It was said that from the walkway running around the tank city lights could be seen all the way to the river. The ladder going up was rickety and a few rungs were missing, but not a few daredevils had made the ascent and recounted the experience with relish.

"I'd like to see what's so spectacular," said Margaret.

"Then get someone to take you up in a plane."

"Oh, no, then you're all closed in. I want to breathe the air!"

Margaret finally sweet-talked Mat into it and they drove up the winding hills to the tower. As they got out of the car Pudge said, "I'll go first." Probably it seemed to him that the bravado of this tilting climb was nothing compared to his trying to fly his coupe over the creek.

"I'll come behind you," said Margaret. "Then Mat, so if I fall," she smiled sweetly, "you can catch me."

"You don't really intend to do this," said Mat.

"I made you bring me, didn't I?"

"What about you, Amy?"

"Nothing doing. I'm staying on the ground."

One by one, ten feet apart, they scaled the shaky ladder, and pulled themselves onto the walkway. The lights of the city shown round about them like diamonds and rubies, and Margaret let out a gleeful squeal.

"Quiet," said Mat. "I know some boys who got arrested doing this."

The excitement was short-lived. When Margaret looked down she got cold feet. Biting her lip she said, "I don't think I can go down."

"Then what the devil do you expect me to do," said Mat, "get the fire department?"

"Mat..."

"You've got to climb down. Just hold tight and look straight ahead."

"Yeah," said Pudge. "I don't think either of us could carry you on our backs."

Finally, with a bit of cursing and tough persuasion Margaret was coaxed down, rung by rung, until they were on terra firma at last. Amy, who had stood beside the car straining her neck to look up, gave her a disgusted glance. "I hope that satisfies you Miss Priss. I could just see three broken bodies at my feet."

After I swore not to say anything, Pudge told me all about this foolhardy climb, but how Margaret's family heard about it no one knew. Very likely Margaret couldn't resist talking to her friends and it got back to the Howells within days. When I heard that the parents were furious with Mat and blamed him for everything, I thought they must be blind. But I had to admit it was stupid for him to let her court disaster this way.

I made every effort not to be in the car when Mat and Margaret faced off, and of course he hated me for being there. At first I admired him for taking the blame, but when he began to understand that her parents had accused him of being "rotten to the core," and "of common stock," he became furious. I was furious, too. In my heart I knew my hard-working, honest, patriotic family was ten times better than the Howells or the Sterlings would ever be.

This time in their fight I heard something different. There was a sort of subterranean, not-quite-focused realization that their clashes were inevitable, circumstances made worse by forces within themselves, and ultimately not worth the agony.

"It was a stupid damn thing for us to do, Margaret. But why in hell did you let your old man know?"

"I didn't say a thing!"

"No? Not a word to anybody."

"Well, maybe one or two girls. But they would never say anything."

"Oh, hell no, of course not."

"Anyway, they know now, and they're being just impossible."

"Tell them to go hang themselves."

"Mat!"

"They're just full of crap, you know. All of them. Maybe you'd better run home to Mama and tell her to pick you a nice boy who don't know his ass from a hole in the ground."

Of course by now Margaret was in tears, and I was close to crying, too. Mat's temper was explosive and I trembled to think of the pain his affair with Margaret was bound to bring him.

* * *

As Daddy and Uncle Talbot continued to hammer, saw, rip, jack up, and bang away at the looming old white two-story, the grotesque pathetic garage out back seemed to squat dead and remote, as though curiously subdued by the disruptive activity. It made me wonder if the unnatural powers of evil could actually be silenced by human forces. In an unsettling way I felt that I was about to lose something.

Whatever it was in that Frankenstein place knew me by name, had identified me as a boy riding a bicycle, and I began to wonder if some sort of appeal to be left alone would have any influence, if I could somehow spark in that black hole a pinpoint of pity. And I kept remembering that once, just once, as we drove by late one night I saw a glimmer of light through the cracked doors. For some reason, I felt I had no choice but to keep up the line of communication.

I didn't know what to say. Finally, on a school paper I wrote my fourth note, and as usual chose a clear afternoon to slip it into the slit in the garage doors. For a week I watched for a response. When none appeared I began to release a slow sigh of relief. It seemed as if I must have struck a sympathetic nerve, and this would be the last of it. My first note had said, *I'm not scared of you!* And this one, pathetically, *We're all scared,* and this time I signed, *Skeeter.* The absence of an answer brought relief but also a kind of lonely confusion.

* * *

As though overnight, when no one noticed, the weather broke, and spring was upon us. Robins flitted and squabbled all over the neighborhood, squirrels ran in insane circles and loops up and down trees. Folding papers, I took off with a new spark around my route, sliding the editions down the sidewalks and onto porches with a deadly, accurate swing of my arm and a snap of the wrist. I knew exactly where the papers, arcing up, curving down, would turn and descend, aiming two or three feet left or right of the landing zone. My old Schwinn, struggling on its last legs, became some animal thing, yielding to my commands like a young stallion. Even getting out of bed was easier with no cold floors to scamper across. This burst of new life when shrubs and trees were unfurling russets and greens evoked an electric energy, though this energy did nothing to soften Daddy's turmoil at the store or my worries. Spring was a time when Mat and his princess should have much to swoon over, but I couldn't see that the singing birds cracked the chill between them, especially in view of her parents' threat to send her away for the summer, and it did not ease my fear of the disaster I believed Mat was getting himself into with Margaret.

One morning several of us arrived in our classroom early and stood around the pencil sharpener talking and looking out the windows. I noticed that Miss Barton had pamphlets and brochures spread across her desk to be examined, and it struck me that in just a few weeks I would no longer be her pupil. This was a bittersweet realization. I would cease to fear her exacting demands and stern glance, but I would never again sit in the light of her charitable knowledge which she so determinedly shared with us.

I had no idea that Miss Barton was aware of my looking over her shoulder until without raising her head she said suddenly, "Come over here, Skeeter."

I crept forward, half curious, half unnerved. Before her, pictures of spires, of swans on lakes, of cathedrals and blooming fields caught my vision in a way that aroused my excitement for far-off places. "Belgium," she said. "Do you know where that is?"

"Europe?"

"Yes. A great part of Europe has suffered terrible destruction from the war but they will find the courage to rebuild. And Belgium is such a lovely place." She slid some of the pamphlets closer to me. "Would you like to travel, Skeeter?"

I hesitated, knowing how much such possibilities were beyond my reach. "Someday." I bent down to look at structures and streets and houses that were different from anything I'd ever seen. "I'd get lost," I mumbled.

"You may. But don't be afraid of adventure. Fear of the unknown can prevent your reaching the things of which you're capable." She glanced up, smiled, and said, as though she knew I would not understand now, but would remember later, "Don't be afraid to chase your dreams. *He who never climbed never fell.*"

The bell rang, we all fell into our desks. For ten minutes I couldn't get my mind on the lesson. I knew I was not her best pupil, but I sensed that she saw something in me. She understood that on the blackest, darkest, most bitter days I'd deliver papers to cold houses as I had promised to do, that my heart went out to people like Jack, that I was restless with visions and desires I could not identify. Whether she understood my fear of every threat lurking around every corner I couldn't say. But it occurred to me that just as in my mind I might travel to wonderful worlds like Belgium and Africa and the Virgin Isles, I could in my mind also erect curtains of fear that would prevent my ever realizing those visions or taking chances. So as with the evil old garage I saw my escape from Miss Barton with relief but also with yet another kind of sadness.

15

Exactly what triggered the breakup between Mat and Margaret I never knew. Perhaps it was the fateful climb up the dangerous water tower, which Margaret precipitated but for which Mat received blame. I didn't at this time understand about girls or care much for them, but it did occur to me that some beautiful rich girls could be cajoling and manipulative. Or it may have been the impending threat of Margaret getting sent away for the summer. Her parents couldn't very well prevent the two sweethearts from seeing each other at school or on band trips or sports events, but they could strategize a summer without dates — disastrous prospects for sixteen-year-olds. Or it may have been what I anticipated all along — that Margaret's lifelong indoctrination into the social circles, her taking her canary yellow Cadi bird as a matter of course, in comparison to our old Chevy and tiny two-bedroom on Schaul — and her increasing awareness of the rewards of marrying sophisticated and rich — in time began to dull her infatuation with Mat.

Whatever it was, I felt certain that the breakup was with harsh words and violent emotions, and for two weeks Mat moped like a man doomed to death. I tiptoed around as if walking a maze of broken eggshells, but I surmised that I'd been wrong about the disastrous effect the end of this relationship would have on him.

I finally broke the somber silence by muttering, "I'm sorry about Margaret, Mat."

He set his jaw, his face masked and inscrutable, and he replied grimly, "No girl's worth dying for."

I imagined that someday he'd meet a girl he did feel was worth dying for, but now it was a great relief to me that within a few weeks his attention was snagged by a black-haired beauty who sang in the Columbus High girls chorus. Why, I wondered, had I wasted so much precious energy in fear of what this breakup would do to Mat? What life groans were wrung out of me when all the time his protective shield was guarding him from emotional disaster!

As I threw papers and mowed lawns—yard care picked up in spring—and each week put a few dollars in my treasury, I chastised myself for harboring such deep fears for my brother; yet I reckoned they were not entirely abated. He still had a temper, he still was driven by devils unknown, but I saw that this was a bridge I'd crossed unnecessarily.

* * *

Every few weeks Daddy and Uncle Talbot resumed work on the gloomy old house on Henry and Francis. They had underpinned the sagging porches and interior floors, removed and replaced rotted cornices and were now in the process of ripping out and repairing windowsills. The big two-story was spotted with new unpainted wood and jagged streaks of old white paint, like a chalk game on concrete walkways. Each time Daddy told us he was going to work there a cold fear came over me. I wanted to go with him and try to help, mostly to keep vigil, but with school, paper route, collecting, homework and yard work, there was almost no time.

When Mr. Preston posted a "For Sale" sign out front I shuddered. How he could dare offer the demon-possessed house to any innocent buyer I couldn't grasp. I could only hope that Daddy and Uncle Talbot wouldn't be blamed for their part in making the awful monster presentable and in a curious way attractive.

Then evil did strike. One night Daddy came home from work and in the same somber tone Mat had assumed following his breakup with Margaret said, "Monty's closing the store. I thought it was just a matter of time."

Mother, stunned, gasped, "But—what happened?"

"Somebody squealed, I think. One of the inspectors on post got nailed and he's spilling the beans to save his own hide. A bunch of plainclothesmen spent all afternoon in the store."

"You know Blaise Montgomery's too slick to keep anything incriminating there," Mama said scornfully.

"I don't know. All the doors were closed but store scuttlebutt's that they were ransacking the books."

"I hope he gets what he deserves."

Mother was the most forgiving, nonjudgmental person in the world, and any vengeful words from her were totally out of character; but it seemed to me she'd earned the right for this accusation. Mr. Montgomery had denied Daddy a raise or even a decent salary, we children suffered while Monty lived high on deceit and fraud, and now, no doubt with a fortune squirreled away that no one would ever find, he could close the doors to Chattahoochee Paint and it would be his employees who'd suffer.

Daddy dropped one shoulder. "He'll buy himself off. Hire a lawyer. Swear he knew nothing about it. Pay a fine and walk away."

"He should be thrown into prison." said Mama.

"That'll never happen."

"But why would he have to close the store?" I asked.

"I guess it's no longer useful to him as a front."

In almost a whisper Mama said, "What're we going to do?"

"I don't know." Daddy shook his head sadly. Then with a spark of optimism he said, "Maybe I'll open my own store. You never get anywhere working for somebody else."

"Yes? With what?"

"There may be a way." He stood and picked up his toolbox. "And this repair business will pay the mortgage. At least I don't have to work under anybody's thumb." His tone was optimistic.

"I hate that you have to work nights and weekends, Daddy," I said. "You never have time for anything." It had never occurred to me that hammer and saw, mostly solitary work, provided him a kind of reprieve.

"I have Sundays, Skeeter," he said. "One day's more than some men have. Besides, I reckon we could go out and live on the farm."

"You mean Grandmother's?"

"Wouldn't that be lovely," Mama said with disgust.

As Daddy slipped on his coat and started out, I hurried after him. "You aren't going back to that house on Henry, are you?"

He nodded. "We're trying to finish up."

"That's where all the trouble comes from."

He paid no attention and I went back into the house and sank down over the arm of a chair. That Daddy might lose his job was not unanticipated but it still was a shock. This was our home for better or worse, and the possibility of getting uprooted was terrifying. There was hardly any chance that I wouldn't have to bring out my savings, abandoning the slightest possibility of a new bike.

Mother came in and sank down on the sofa, the spent padding concaving to her weight like a sponge ball. Joanie looked up from the floor. "What's wrong, Mommy?"

As though realizing how even her expressions affected our two-year-old, Mama said, "You know, Joanie, I think I have ingredients for chocolate fudge. Why don't we make some now?"

I fell right in. "Yes, let's do, Joanie. We'll help."

I took her hand and led her to the kitchen.

* * *

In the morning I passed by Malcolm's house just as he came out and we walked to school together. I was glad for a chance to talk, though I didn't know what to say or even if I should say anything. My parents wanted neither pity nor charity, but it was embarrassing for me that we were so broke.

Kicking solemnly at tufts of grass and tree roots, I mumbled, "My daddy lost his job last night. As soon as they close the store he'll be out of work."

Malcolm didn't slow his stride. "What's he going to do?"

"We don't know. Look for work. But jobs are hard to find."

"Yeah. My brother's finished school and he's asking around. No takers so far."

"He's talked about opening his own store or trying to do more remodeling with Uncle Talbot." I hefted my books to the left side. "If only Daddy hadn't started working on that old house."

"You think that's why he's having trouble?

"Maybe he was getting too close."

"Yeah, I bet that's it." Malcolm's voice assumed a peculiar uplift, faintly devious. "You never know what'll come out of that dungeon."

"Why would it come after us, though?" I protested. "We're just trying to make a living."

"Maybe it's something you did, Skeeter."

"Me!" I stumbled, spinning toward him. "What did I do?"

"What about those notes?"

"But it was your idea!"

"Not really. I just encouraged you to do *something*."

Outraged, I cried, "If you hadn't made me look through those doors — !"

"That wouldn't have mattered. You'd be just as scared." With a touch of pity he said, "All right, maybe it wasn't you. I probably would've done something too if I thought it'd make me feel better."

I had a sneaking suspicion Malcolm knew something he wasn't telling. I remembered he had implied some hazy acquaintance with the people in the big white house. "Who are they, anyway?" I said. "How can they live so near that garage?"

"I don't know. Maybe they're part of it."

I thought of the people I'd seen on the porch, of Mr. Preston, and the thin white arm that appeared to wave or motion to me. "Maybe whatever's in that hole isn't that mean," I said. "Those messages—the answers—seemed kinda sad."

"Sad?"

"It didn't even answer the last time."

"What'd you say?"

"Not much. Just something about being scared. We have a right to be."

"Well," Malcolm observed conspiratorially, "maybe he's scared, too."

"What could he be scared of?"

"Who knows? Maybe just getting out of there."

This was a completely new idea to me. I felt an irrational urge to head straight to the old garage, burst through the doors and confront the threat face to face. But I didn't dare. Was it possible that opening the door to my prison might reveal nothing worth the anguish I had invested in it?

16

The proverbs Miss Barton wrote on the chalk board that I remembered most were *Don't cut off your nose to spite your face*, *Look before you leap*, and *Haste makes waste*. These spears of advice were to challenge me often, and when disobeyed took their own personal vengeance. Her proverbs never failed to hit their mark and never failed in one piercing jab to divulge the wisdom of books. I guess these proverbs and *The Adventures of Remi* were her trademark, her legacy, and neither could ever betray those who followed her.

It seemed to me Miss Barton's step became brisker, her gestures more animated. It could have been spring, which energized us all. It could have been that we were coming to the close of another school year and she felt pleased and successful with our class. I was pretty certain not every group of pupils carried the same weight of accomplishment. It may have been her plans to travel during the summer and the exciting preparation for it. To me her step had always been purposeful and intent, now it transmitted the snappy march of a majorette. Her expression was aglow and girl-like—or so it seemed to me. I realized that this, too, might just have been an impression I derived from my own sense of escape. My fears of her sharp tongue and clipped demands were greatly abated, and in just a few weeks I would be out of her class forever.

This was a bittersweet revelation. I thought in my fifth grade class I had learned everything I'd ever need to know. I'm sure not every pupil who fell under her scathing scrutiny came away as mature and enlightened as I believed I was. I wanted to be away from school, to be out of classrooms forever, to go my way, to use my intelligence as best I could and to use the education Miss Barton and others before her had imparted to me. Then again, I feared passing through this sheltered life and orderly regimen when intelligence and education would not be enough, and I'd yearn to listen to the teacher's reading of *Remi*. I guess every child at some time feels that way—desperate to grow up but fearing the unknowns where all kinds of dangers lurked.

No matter what, I felt I'd never cease to make use of Miss Barton's proverbs, those timeless gems of wisdom, or cease to appreciate this special teacher of Wynnton School and her passion to teach.

* * *

Summers are not a good time for birthdays. School is out, families are traveling, camps are underway, kids miss out on parties. So we celebrated my birthday on the last Saturday before the end of fifth grade class. Our house was too small, and our backyard, with its scorched garage, patches of dirt, and remnants of Daddy's construction projects, was not a festive place, to say the least. But this made no difference to neighborhood kids, who were in and out all the time, or to cousins who paid no attention. We could look forward to the big school-time parties of well-off classmates at the Cherokee Lodge or one of the country retreats.

In July, I would turn eleven—a high moment, for it brought me one year closer to twelve, when I would be grown, independent, wise, mature, and capable of making it on my own. Then several things happened to spoil my excitement. Mat announced that he thought he'd attend my party. He had never shown his face at any of them before, usually making himself scarce, and what possessed him I couldn't imagine. I only knew I didn't want him there. He'd tease us, make fun of everything, and generally treat us like babies. He would embarrass me before my cousins and friends, and I would be the brunt of his harassment.

"Don't let him come, Mama." I appealed to my mother's sense of fairness. "He can just stay at work."

"Of course, your brother should come to your party if he wants to."

"He'll just pick on us. He hates me."

"Of course he doesn't hate you."

"He thinks I'm a pain."

"Maybe you don't know what he thinks. He could show you how to have fun. Most kids like older kids."

"It's my party. I should be able to invite who I want."

Unsuccessful in enlisting Mama's influence, I tried to persuade Mat. "You wouldn't like it. You'll think our games are silly."

He grinned tauntingly. "What'll you do? Spin the bottle? Throw darts blindfolded? Maybe I'll teach you how to pitch pennies."

"I don't gamble like you, Mat."

This argument continued for two or three days, until finally I cried spitefully, "I don't want you at my party! You'll just ruin it."

He answered nonchalantly, "Maybe I'll practice my trumpet. Some sad funeral marches." But I was surprised to see that my words wounded him.

Then on Saturday morning I took off early to collect for the paper, hoping my old Schwinn would not let me down. I wanted to finish as quickly as possible, get back home, and enjoy some time before my party. As usual, though, collecting did not go smoothly and it was early afternoon that I finally turned toward home. I veered off Thirteenth, cruised down Wynnton, and wheeled down Henry. At once I saw plastered across Mr. Preston's "For Sale" sign a big bold "Sold!" Someone had bought the haunted house! There would be new occupants, innocent victims who probably had no awareness of what they were letting themselves into. Not only were the front door and downstairs windows thrown open, the upstairs windows, where tight curtains had always remained drawn, were also uncurtained and raised high. It was as if some bizarre current had whipped through to leave the occupants stripped of disguise and to render me aghast.

As if this weren't shock enough, as I passed the house I received the second, more startling one. The old garage was gone. Gone! Demolished! Swept away! Vanished as though it had never existed! I nearly fell off my bike. With something akin to shellshock I pulled up to a graveyard of broken and abandoned things—shards of wood and roofing, machine parts, remnants of tools and paint, furniture pieces, a rusty old spring chair, and even old bicycle parts, sprockets and chains and grips, almost a mirror image of our own garage on Schaul.

On tense and straining legs I parked my bike at the curb and began to skulk through the debris, inhaling the biting odor of mold and decay smoldering and disseminating like a burned-out trash pile. The rusty spring chair remained exactly where it must have sat for years, and I realized that this was the precise position it had commanded the time I peeked through the doors to detect the faint glow of a cigarette. My glance shifted with bullet speed to assimilate the broken blocks which had been the foundation wall, the hard-as-concrete black dirt floor, an old bicycle fender, the remnants of useless junk which had made up the bowels of this tomb of torture as I had imagined it. How could this have happened? It was as though some tornadic force had thundered through to sweep away forever the evil that had resided there. For five minutes I stood with mouth agape. Finally it occurred to me that, dilapidated as the old structure was, a demolition crew with sledgehammer and crowbar and dump truck could dismantle and remove the shattered remains in hours.

As I kicked at pieces of useless junk, the cat I'd seen sunning on the rotted fence came tiptoeing through, sniffing step by tender step, as though it, too, sought some cosmic explanation—sought in vain, for there was not so much as two pieces of wall held together to suggest an earlier dwelling. For all my years of terror all I got now was startling anticlimax, letdown and a peculiar resentment.

Disappointed, I finally broke away and hurried home, trying to put the spooky garage behind me, trying not to dread Mat's badgering but excited about my afternoon party. Mama was in the kitchen making the cake, Joanie guiding her doll buggy carefully around dining room table and chairs.

I knew some of my aunts and uncles would probably give me money for my birthday and decided to go to my closet and look at how much my cache had grown. I hadn't done this for several weeks, but I knew exactly how many bills I had, ones and fives and tens. I placed the foil-covered box on the dresser and opened the lid slowly, savoring the moment. Then I just stood staring. One of my tens was gone! I had three, and now there were only two! I'd been robbed!

I stood furious and speechless. How many shocks was I to receive in one day! Then I slammed the box aside and ran to the kitchen. "Mat's taken my money!"

Mother hardly seemed to hear.

"Ten dollars! He's taken my money!"

"What are you talking about, Skeeter?"

"Mat took it! He's the only one who could have."

"Nonsense. Go look again."

"I don't need to look. I had three tens…" I began to rattle off each denomination. "Where is he! I want my money!"

"He went to work early. He's trying to make overtime."

During summers, with people traveling, service stations pumped more gas, cleaned more windshields, washed more cars, and sandblasted more sparkplugs. This was the time Mat could get in extra work. I slipped a comb through my hair and started out.

"Where are you going?" Mama asked.

"To get my ten dollars!"

"You'll do nothing of the kind. You won't make a scene at his work."

"Why would he take my money!"

"If your brother took your money it must have been for a loan or something. He'll put it back."

"He didn't even ask me!"

"Maybe because you were asleep. I told you he left early. You can ask him when he comes home for your party."

"Oh damn!"

"Skeeter! You will not say words like that."

The words I could have used were much worse. I wanted to call Mat but knew I couldn't without Mother hearing. That my own brother would take my money, even for a loan, without asking, was incomprehensible to me. If he'd asked and there had been some urgent need like helping Daddy, I would have given it to him. I wondered if he'd gotten into some sort of trouble, if maybe something could have happened with Margaret. I wondered if he'd eloped! I had an idea mother wasn't telling all she knew.

I went out and closed the garage doors to hide the junk, cleaned up around the back porch, swept the steps, and pulled the few remaining dry clothes off the clothesline. Every time I thought about my missing money I became sick. Finally, around four in the afternoon, the kids began to arrive and we all funneled into the backyard, the best place for parties in the summer. We were running and shouting and flying about like scattered crows when I heard Mat come home. At once I grew tense. The afternoon was about to be spoiled. The car door slammed, he yelled to Mama from the kitchen.

I was poised to receive his barbs as he burst through the rear screened porch. I wanted to yell, "Where is my money!" but knew it would spoil everything. I held my breath, but what happened next totally confounded me. Mat came bounding out and simply commandeered the party. In minutes all my friends and cousins were laughing, catching him by the arm, swinging and gathering around him. Much as I had dreaded his arrival, he was pumping life into my celebration, creating pinnacles of laughter as though there could be nothing he enjoyed more than taking us under his wing. Shamed but too excited to interrupt the wild excitement, I felt elevated in the eyes of the others to have produced this windfall in the form of a brother. I could hardly comprehend it.

"Mat!" they cried, "Watch this!" and, "Show me, Mat! Show me!"

We played hard for an hour, and then from the back porch Mama called, "Don't you want to come on in and open presents, Skeeter?"

Almost in chorus everyone yelled, "Yes!"

We scrambled through the kitchen into the living room. The presents were stacked in the middle of the floor. I sat down with my back against the sofa, the others standing or squatting around me, Mat and Mama perching on chairs pulled out from the dining room table, and Joanie wobbling back and forth among presents and tissue wrappings. I removed ribbons and paper meticulously, taking time, enjoying the suspense. A new Monopoly set, a whole case of B-B's for my Daisy, a small portable radio which I could take on my paper route to keep me company. From Mama and Daddy I received a front fender light for my bicycle, a sleeping bag that would be much warmer than my old one, some outdoor cooking equipment, some badly needed underwear. The comments were typical. "Aw, how nice." "Thank you, I love this." "I got one just like that for my birthday."

When the last present was unwrapped and stacked at the end of the sofa we had our usual cake and ice cream, I thanked everybody again, and my eleventh birthday party was over.

* * *

Just as the last guest left Mat said, "I have something for you, Skeeter."

I hadn't even noticed that there has been no present from him. "What is it?"

"We'll have to go see."

I glanced inquiringly at Mama and she gave me a brief nod.

"Where're we going?"

"C'mon, I'll show you."

We went out and got into the car. Mat backed out onto Schaul, turned left on Henry, and drove straight to the big white house whose backyard looked strange to me now that the evil garage had been torn down. He pulled up to the front of the house and parked.

Tersely I said, "You don't have to tease me, Mat. What kind of joke is this."

"It's not a joke." He tapped the horn in some kind of sequence. "Get out."

Tense and uncertain, I walked up onto the big front porch with him. Just as we reached the top step the door swung open and I stopped dead still. A tall, white-complexioned young man of about thirty came out, looked at me with a shy smile, and extended his hand.

"I want you to meet Mr. Napp Zimmerman." Mat gave me a wink, as if to say, "your spook." "I think you've already met him indirectly."

I embarrassed myself by staring. In Napp Zimmerman's pale face his eyes were incredibly blue, his knuckles almost unpigmented white, and his lips a mottled pink-red. He had sparse hair, a narrow chest, and arms almost as white as the dingy white of the unpainted backdrop of boards. While his appearance was strange, his movements and gestures were graceful, almost swanlike, and I thought there was something gentle and pensive about him. He held out his hand and said, "Hullo, Skeeter."

The instant our hands touched a bright blaze of clarity flashed over me. Incomprehensibly, I blurted, "It was you!"

Mat said authoritatively, "Napp's an artist. Portraits, mostly, I believe."

Still in a flash of enlightenment I murmured, "He drew a picture of me—he has a pretty handwriting, too."

In his grownup tone Mat said, "Napp doesn't get out much. He's allergic to the sun. The allergy is called solar urticaria."

"The sun," I echoed, like a parrot.

"His skin doesn't like sunlight and he remains inside mostly."

"You don't live in the garage?" I said dumbly.

"I work out there at night," smiled Napp, "and sometimes slip out during the day to get away from my studio a while."

"But how did you know him, Mat? Tell me what's going on."

"Oh, I almost forgot—your birthday present."

They both grinned and Napp turned, walked through the front door into the big foyer, and rolled out a beautiful Schwinn bicycle. Again, I stood stark cold. At first I thought it was a new bike, then I realized that it was Mat's bicycle completely rebuilt—new sprockets, new seat and tires, special handlebars, and a beautiful paint job with racing stripes and my initials on the frame. Finally, I cried "Mat!" Tears came into my eyes—tears of shock, of joy, of shame." I'd been so ugly to him. "How could you—"

"I knew this is what you wanted more than anything, and I was determined you'd have it. I didn't have quite enough money to finish up and had to slip a ten from you. I knew that's what you wanted to do with it."

I opened my mouth to breathe, swallowed, a catch in my voice. "I'm sorry, Mat."

He seemed not to hear. "But I was only part of it," he said. "Really, Napp did it all. It was his idea and he did all the work."

"Napp?"

The young man smiled shyly. "I rebuild bikes for needy kids. I found out about you and with your brother's help was able to pull it off."

"You rebuilt Mat's old bike—and made it look like this!"

"I did. I hope you like it."

"It's the prettiest Schwinn I've ever seen. Better than any new one. But how did you find out about me?"

"Malcolm."

"Malcolm!"

"The minute you wrote the first note he told me all about you."

"He never even let on he knew you!"

Napp's grin broadened. "We're cousins."

"Cousins!" I repeated dumbly.

"Our families are related by marriage."

I had an urge to kill. Looking down at my shoes, I murmured, "And I was so afraid of the garage…I guess I made it all up." I felt like crawling into a hole. That the evil spirit I'd feared was this tall, washed-out young man with a shy smile and unfortunate circumstances in his life…How deeply he understood my fears I didn't know, but I doubted that he had any idea how I was drawn to him even in my terror. I realized somehow that the old shack had been useful in my mind as something I could blame for my fears, something that just came from my head.

I said, "I'm sorry about your sickness."

"It's okay, Skeeter. I just have to be careful."

"Do you ever get out?"

"When it's cloudy, rainy. My skin is hypersensitive but I wear full clothing."

"It must be hard."

"In summer especially I look out and see you kids riding,…"

"I don't know if I could stand being indoors all the time."

"It could be worse. I have my work. Painting and the bikes. And there are medicines that help."

It all felt strange. For a long time in my mind the old garage had been occupied by something inhuman and wicked. And here was my evil spirit who had spent weeks or months making something for me I might never have gotten without him. I felt ashamed. Perhaps I stood on the verge of liberation, but mostly I wished I had been able to reach out to this bone-white man who must miss companionship that I took for granted. Weeks ago, I would have rejoiced in the demolition of the old garage and people leaving the house; now I was sorry to see them go.

"It was stupid for me to be afraid of that shack," I said.

Napp smiled again. "I wouldn't regret that, Skeeter. Sometimes it's fun to imagine things and I enjoyed our little mystery, too. Perhaps, though, the things we most fear never occur."

"But the old garage has been torn down. What'll you do now?"

"At our new house I'll have a special studio. No more climbing upstairs."

Mat said, "I gotta go to work. Trying to make overtime."

"To spend on me," I mumbled.

I felt happy and bad. I tried to dab my eyes without them seeing. There was a smudge on the front fender and with my handkerchief I carefully wiped it off. White stripes on blue was my favorite and it had a good, sturdy chain guard, too. How long that would last I couldn't guess, but at least for a while I wouldn't come home with greasy, tooth-chewed pant cuffs.

I'd never hugged my brother, I had never told him I loved him. I couldn't imagine anything more awkward. But as he bounded down the steps I ran and caught his arm. "Thank you for my bicycle, Mat."

"Don't be afraid to use it. Nothing stays new forever."

"I know. I won't be afraid." I watched him drive off. As I walked back up the stairs I thought I'd been the victim of a three-way conspiracy—Malcolm, Mat and the kind and gentle spook, Napp Zimmerman. And Malcolm had started it all. I wanted to hug him and kill him.

Napp said, "I guess I'd better get back inside." He held out his hand. "I'm glad to meet you, Skeeter. I feel I've known you for a long time."

Before I could say anything, he disappeared into the house. I pushed my bike slowly down the steps. Had it not been for my irrational fears I might have gotten to know Napp Zimmerman better. He had devoted all that time and thought to making a present for me. That would never happen now, and the only way I knew not to blame myself was to concentrate on plotting the most painful way to kill Malcolm Hughley.

* * *

Malcolm never let me come close to killing him. The minute I cried, "You tricked me!" he laughed.

"You tricked yourself, Skeeter, I just encouraged you."

"He's your cousin!" I insisted.

"So - so - distant."

I was unrelenting. "Evil spirit, huh? You must have had a big laugh, Malcolm."

He shrugged. "Why're you griping? You're so scary-scary, the old garage gave you something to blame it on."

"Well, I'm not now," I said boldly. "It was just stupid."

We were sitting on his front steps. Jean and Johnny came by and we waved to them. One of them said something and they both giggled.

"I guess you talked Napp Zimmerman into going along."

"I didn't talk him into anything. When you stuck that first note in the door I told him you and some of the other kids thought the garage was haunted. It gave him something to enjoy, too."

I decided it wouldn't really help to kill Malcolm. I looked down at my shoes, which needed new soles. "How anyone could ever think Napp could be evil. I feel sorry for him."

"It was never somebody you were afraid of," said Malcolm. "It was always something you imagined."

"But I had hateful thoughts and all it was, was a place for him to get away awhile. I wish you'd told me, Malcolm."

"That would've messed it up."

I felt like crying. "I wish I could stop being afraid all the time. The stuff that happens to us ..."

"Look, Skeeter." Malcolm, who was twelve and already knew everything, decided to be nice. "How many kids you think could handle that big paper route you have? In the freezing cold. Pitch dark Sunday mornings and nobody on the street but you. It'd scare the pee outa me, but you do it."

I looked over to see if he was baiting me, but he was serious.

"I'd say you're pretty brave. And all that other stuff you're afraid of—you can just decide to forget it."

It seemed then that the most appropriate attitude for me to take was one of sentimentality. "It's kind of sad that the old garage is gone. Everything's changing."

"Yeah," said Malcolm. "Someday paperboys won't even ride bikes. They'll all have their own cars. Postmen, too."

"I hope so. I'd hate for my kids to have to do what I do."

He gave me a jab with his elbow. "It's made a man of you. You just don't get it yet."

I stood, stretched, and ran home, sailing over roots and patches of grass like blowing leaves.

* * *

I did not get to say goodbye to Napp Zimmerman. The spooky old garage had been torn down, Daddy and Uncle Talbot were putting the finishing touches on the house, new people were preparing to move in. Daddy was upbeat about a new remodeling job they had contracted for, and about the possibility of opening his own hardware store. With my newfound courage I intended to walk up to the door of the old white house and ask Napp or his parents if I could come in. But I didn't have a chance. Just a few days after my Saturday birthday celebration I was heading up to Wynnton to throw my papers when I saw a big moving van pulling away from the Zimmerman house. Behind the van was a car with shaded windows. As I slowed to watch them pass a back window rolled down and Napp threw his arm up to me. "Goodbye, Napp!" I yelled. "Thank you!" He smiled and nodded.

I folded my papers, stuffed them into the canvas bag and strapped the bag to the handlebars of my beautiful streamlined Schwinn. I jumped on and rode fast and smoothly, the wind blowing my hair, careful of the ditches and curbs, but knowing it was only a matter of time before I'd have to put my blue and white steed through the ropes. It was the way I made my money and helped my family out a little. I knew I wouldn't be afraid anymore of potholes, or ditches, or unknowns lurking around dark corners.

Acknowledgments

To my readers who have supported my work, all royalties from the sale of my books are used to help those in need, thus you have become a part of that. My thanks to Sue B. Walker and Negative Capability Press, one of the South's oldest literary publishers; to Nick Norwood, Scott Wilkerson, and Allen Gee for their editorial input; and most of all, to my wife, Sara who remained patient through hundreds of hours as I anguished over the typewriter.

About the Author

Donald Jordan is the founder of the Donald L. Jordan Prize for Literary Excellence, whose mission is "to encourage and promote writings which honor the traditional values of responsibility, gratitude, generosity, love and faith." He lives and works in Columbus, Georgia and has written two other novels, *Happy Lightning*, *Negative Space*, and a work of nonfiction, *The Creation: A Letter*.